"First it's the green light,
then the cold shoulder. I don't know
where I am with you."

"I . . . I don't understand . . ." she choked.

"I thought I was making myself abysmally
clear," Nick growled.

Trembling, she shook her head, too confused to
speak. She felt strangely helpless. Very slowly,
he bent towards her, his eyes turning almost
black as he searched her face before letting his
lips meet hers, tentatively, asking silent questions. Unable to help herself, she swayed towards him in instinctive invitation, guilty pleasure shivering through her as he took her
tightly in his arms.

Bantam Circle of Love Romances
Ask your bookseller for the books you have missed

GOLD IN HER HAIR by Anne Neville
ROYAL WEDDING by Mary Christopher
DESIGN FOR ENCHANTMENT
by Rachel Murray
THE HEATHER IS WINDBLOWN
by Anne Saunders
GATES OF THE SUN by Lucinda Day
A RING AT THE READY by Anna West
ASHTON'S FOLLY by Jean Innes
THE RELUCTANT DAWN
by Juliet Lawrence
THE CINDERELLA SEASON
by Elaine Daniel

Dear Friend,

Enter the Circle of Love—and travel to faraway places with romantic heroes. . .

We read hundreds of novels and, each month, select the very best—from the finest writers around the world—to bring you these wonderful love stories . . . stories that let *you* share in a variety of beautiful romantic experiences.

With Circle of Love Romances, you treat yourself to a romantic holiday—anytime, anywhere. And because we want to please you, won't you write and let us know your comments and suggestions?

Meanwhile, welcome to the Circle of Love— we don't think you'll ever want to leave!

Best,

Cathy Camhy
Editor

CIRCLE OF LOVE

Royal Wedding

Mary Christopher

BANTAM BOOKS
TORONTO · NEW YORK · LONDON · SYDNEY

ROYAL WEDDING

A Bantam Book / April 1982

CIRCLE OF LOVE, the garland and the ring designs.
are trademarks of Bantam Books, Inc.

ISBN 0-553-21507-8

Published simultaneously in the United States and Canada.

Bantam Books are published by Bantam Books, Inc. Its trade-
mark, consisting of the words "Bantam Books" and the por-
trayal of a rooster, is Registered in U.S. Patent and Trademark
Office and in other countries. Marca Registrada. Bantam
Books, Inc., 666 Fifth Avenue, New York, New York 10103.

PRINTED IN THE UNITED STATES OF AMERICA

0 9 8 7 6 5 4 3 2

For my sons, ANDREW and KEVIN, who are both old enough to be a little in love with the former Lady Diana Spencer.

For MICHAEL RAINES, who helped make a treehouse for the future Princess of Wales.

And for JANET RAE, with many thanks for all the help she gave in the very early stages of this book.

One

Her caller's language made Mrs. John James Elliott blanch and, with a look of pain, remove the receiver from her ear.

"Are you aware to whom you are speaking?" she demanded frostily.

The man hesitated, then said more calmly, "Yes, ma'am, I'm sorry. But I'd hoped to find your daughter with you. It's vitally important that I contact her as soon as possible. If she isn't staying at your house, then where is she?"

"Julie is driving to the New Jersey shore to stay with her grandparents," Mrs. Elliott informed him. "Perhaps you have forgotten, but she *is* supposed to be on vacation. I'll give you the number, but she won't be there for a while yet. Whatever this fuss is all about, it will have to wait."

Having given him the number, she laid down the phone and removed her well-manicured hand as if the instrument had soiled her. Really, it was too bad that Julie had got herself involved with such rough people!

The Elliott family was one of the oldest in Philadelphia, Julie's father a respected lawyer and her mother well known for charitable work. But their only child, Julie Joanna Elliott, had chosen to go into journalism. Her mother despaired of her.

The object of all this anguish was at that moment driving along the coastal highway. Since she was not clairvoyant and had no idea that her life was about to be irrevocably altered, the main thing on her mind was the weather.

She had planned to spend her week's vacation soaking up the summer sun, but even before she left Philadelphia, clouds had been gathering, and now the rain poured down in leaden sheets, almost defeating the sweeps of her windshield wipers. Occasional glimpses of the Atlantic showed slate-gray waves heaving onto a deserted beach, with a single yacht driving for shelter across Barnegat Bay.

A truck roared by, sending up a great shower that momentarily obliterated her view, but when she could see clearly again, she found herself approaching the white blur that could only be the fencing around the park of Red Oaks. Thank heaven for that! She eased her foot onto the brake and turned between open gates onto a driveway that curved among trees.

The house to which her grandparents had retired several years before was a white sprawling mansion set in a broad acreage of lawns dotted with red oaks, which gave the place its name. Through windblown mists of rain, Julie saw the familiar façade ahead, its steps leading up to the porched main door and verandas now glassed in and green with the plants that Mrs. J. J. Elliott, Sr., loved to fuss over. Julie pulled up by the steps and leaped out into the downpour to throw up the lid of the trunk and take out her suitcase.

"Hello, Julie!" her grandmother called from the porch. "Glad you could make it, dear!"

"I almost got washed away," Julie replied, ducking back into the car to gather a precious pile of magazines from the passenger seat, clutching them awkwardly as she ran for the shelter of the house.

She felt hot, damp and disheveled—and consequently not in the best of moods. In a moment of pure confusion, she attempted, all at the same time, to kiss her grandmother, put down her case, and save the magazines as they threatened to slip from her grasp. She was aware of someone thumping down the stairs as she lost her battle with coordination and two of the magazines went slithering to the floor, to be picked up by a stocky, freckle-faced youth—her cousin Gary, she saw with a sinking heart. Glancing at the glossy covers of the books, Gary gave her a knowing, superior-male grin.

"Don't tell me you're into this royal wedding thing, J. J.? I thought women's lib was more your scene."

More irritated than ever, Julie snatched back the magazines, smoothing the creases from a shiny cover showing the Prince of Wales and his bride-to-be. "A journalist has to be interested in everything," she retorted.

"Huh, the great newspaperwoman," her cousin snorted. "Covering everything—from PTA functions to meetings of the Daughters of the American Revolution."

"It's all news!" Julie said crossly.

"Children!" Mrs. Elliott broke in with an indulgent laugh. "Enough of that. Gary, you take Julie's things up to her room. She'll want to wash up after her trip."

"She looks like she needs it," Gary replied, making a face at Julie, but he picked up her suitcase and went toward the stairs, climbing two at a time.

Mrs. Elliott, elegant in a shirtwaist dress and gold choker, her gray hair neat and curly, turned to wink at Julie. "Take no notice of him, honey. Men don't understand these things. Frankly, I can't wait until July twenty-ninth. I'll be up all night sooner than miss a minute of the ceremony. I've even bought a new dress to wear—even though I'll only be watching it on TV. It's so romantic! Prince Charles is such a charming young man, and his fiancée's sweet. He couldn't have chosen better."

"I guess not," Julie said, adding with a wistfulness that was only half feigned, "Though of course he never got to meet *me*, did he?"

3

"That's his misfortune," her grandmother said, laughing. "Oh, never mind, honey, there are other young men in the world. If you can't have a prince, maybe you'll end up with a lord. How are your parents?"

"Oh, pretty well," Julie replied. "Daddy's involved in some big fraud case, and Mom is up to her eyes with her committees, as usual, but they said they'll come visit you before the summer is over. They love it here. We all do—even in the rain. Is this weather going to improve, do you know?"

"According to the radio, it will be gone by morning," Mrs. Elliott assured her. "Now, why don't you go freshen up, honey? I'll have Helen make some tea."

Having taken a shower and slipped into a shirt and jeans, Julie sat on her bed slowly flipping through the magazines—all special issues concerning the royal engagement and the forthcoming wedding. Pictures of Prince Charles and Lady Diana Spencer smiled from every page; the world's most eligible bachelor had finally succumbed to the snares of love, and most of the women on earth, including Julie, were preparing to shed happy tears for him and his bride.

Most of all, Julie envied the media people who would be gathering in London for the big event. Gary's jibe about PTA meetings had stung her, for it was not far from the truth.

When she had become a journalist, she had imagined herself covering the big stories—being right in there at the scene of fires, or interviewing state senators over hot political issues—but like so many other women beginning in the profession, she had found herself consigned to the Women's Page, doing bits and pieces that seemed hardly worth the trouble of rushing to type "takes" for the harassed copy-readers, who only hacked her careful prose to pieces. Even on the Women's Page, any halfway meaty stories were handled by Julie's senior, Marsha Harris.

If ever Julie had envied Marsha, it was never more so than now, when the older woman was about to jet off to London to cover the royal wedding—which just had to be the most exciting assignment ever. The nearest Julie would come to it would be a TV set in the middle of the night after a hard day slaving to meet the deadline for the morning edition of the *Philadelphia Star.*

Heaving another sigh, she tore herself away from thoughts of what might have been and went to stare out of the window at the lashing rain. The oaks in the park tossed their summer leaves in the storm, and water streamed down the pane. So much for acquiring a swift tan! Depressed, she sat by the mirror and brushed her long hair.

She had once been told that she had typical "English Rose" coloring—tawny-blond hair and green eyes, with dark eyebrows and lashes. The thought pleased her, since she was proud of her English ancestry, though she knew she was no ravishing beauty. However, she was tall and slim, with curves in all the right places, and to judge by men's reaction to her, she wasn't exactly displeasing to their eyes. In her twenty-two years she had encountered most types of men—shy types, hearty types, some who were all hands—but never yet one who had lit that spark, or whatever it was that happened between a man and a woman. The photographs of the soon-to-be-wed royal pair shouted the fact that they had found it. Why didn't it happen to Julie?

"Oh, snap out of it!" she groaned at her reflection, making a face before jumping to her feet. She was supposed to be a modern woman, not a misty-eyed fool, dreaming about princes and happy endings. If Gary guessed that she was becoming obsessed with dreams of romance, he would give her no peace.

"Julie!" Mrs. Elliott was calling. "Julie, dear!"

Julie went out onto the gallery, from where she saw her grandmother smiling from the hall below.

"You've been so long I thought you'd fallen asleep, honey. Helen's made the tea. Come have some before it gets cold."

Afternoon tea was a tradition at Red Oaks, taken the English way ever since the senior Elliotts had visited the old country some years before. It was served in the rear sitting room, beside a marble fireplace, which at present was graced by a tapestry screen woven by an Elliott ancestor. From either side of the hearth, portraits of the original Elliotts looked down on the present generations.

Settling into an easy chair, Julie met the smiling eyes of the first J.J.—Captain John James Elliott, portrayed in his uniform of red coat and tricorn, a gilded ornamental collar around his neck proclaiming his status as an officer. Family tradition said that he had come from England in the eighteenth century, an impoverished younger son of the aristocracy, probably fleeing from the law. He had distinguished himself in the Indian Wars before marrying the wealthy heiress Betty Linstrom, whose picture balanced his on the wall. Caught in hasty strokes by some amateur artist, Betty looked horse faced, with hardly any neck, her pudgy little hands folded beneath the low-cut bosom of a gown the color of mud. But whether the portrait was accurate or not, her wealth must have been ample compensation for bold but penniless John Elliott. The twinkle in his eyes seemed to confirm as much, Julie thought.

She liked the look of her roguish ancestor, who had fathered four children before being killed in the Revolutionary War. Though proud that this adventurous relative of hers had fought for the independence of his adopted land, Julie often wondered wistfully about the home he had left behind in England. She often wished she knew exactly *where*— so that someday she might go back and visit the place. In fact, she had planned to make such a trip the previous year, but an accident to her mother—a broken hip—had prevented her leaving. Now if only she were in Marsha Harris's shoes, going to cover the wedding. . . .

Catching herself slipping back into pointless daydreams, she sat up and turned her mind to reality.

"Where's grandpa gone?" she asked as her grandmother poured tea from an antique silver pot.

"Oh, he went to have someone look at the car," Mrs. Elliott replied. "You know how he is, always imagining some noise or other in the engine. He'll be home any minute. He was looking forward to seeing you. He does like having the family around him. But you must tell me all your news while we've got the chance to talk privately. Gary's in the den watching TV. Some ball game he didn't want to miss."

"Still more interested in sports than studying?" Julie asked, lifting her eyebrows under the wing of hair that fell across her brow.

Mrs. Elliott replied with a glance at the ceiling, as if to say that only intervention from heaven could improve Gary's performance at college. He was supposed to be studying law, in order to join the family firm of Elliott and Elliott, but so far he seemed more keen on chasing a ball than reading law books.

"His parents will be coming over in a day or two," Mrs. Elliott said. "Gary came early to get in some sailing, though he's spent more time out in the beach buggy. I'm hoping your cousin Laurene will be visiting for a few days, too—with her new fiancé. Have you met him?"

"No, not yet," Julie said airily, pretending not to notice the meaningful note in her grandmother's voice.

"I don't suppose you . . ." Mrs. Elliott let the sentence hang unfinished in the air between them.

"Grandma," Julie said firmly, "I'm a career woman. I've only just got started in journalism. No man is going to waylay me, not for a while."

Mrs. Elliott sighed. "I suppose that's the modern way, though I can't pretend to understand it. I met your grandpa when I was younger than you. Isn't there some nice young man in your life?"

"Plenty—but they're all just friends and nothing else." Wanting to change the tone of the conversation, she leaned forward, her eyes dancing. "Besides, I'm on the rebound—I haven't got used to the fact that Prince Charles is out of my reach now."

"Julie!" her grandmother admonished, laughing.

"You can never be serious, can you? But Lady Diana is only nineteen—three years younger than you. Don't wait too long, that's my advice, or all the available men will be snapped up. Maybe your dream man will be on the beach this week."

"Maybe—if the sun let's him come out to play," Julie said lightly, her spirits lifting. She was a free agent, and if some gorgeous man did happen along, she wouldn't try to avoid him.

Out in the hall the phone rang, and the housekeeper answered it, then put her head around the sitting room door to say, "That was Mr. Elliott. Seems he has to leave the car with the mechanic, and he wants someone to go pick him up."

"Oh, my!" Mrs. Elliott said, a hand to her unlined cheek. "So he was right about that rattle in the engine. Julie would you—?"

"Of course," Julie said at once, setting her empty cup on the table.

The rain seemed to have eased a little as she nosed her car out of the driveway, and she congratulated herself on escaping more discussion of matrimony. Her grandmother was a darling, but it seemed she couldn't wait to see Julie—and the rest of her grandchildren—standing at the altar.

When she arrived at the local garage, she saw that her grandfather was sitting having coffee in the snack bar next to the garage. When he saw her pull up, he waved through the window, drained his cup, and came striding out to greet her, still lithe, bronzed, and athletic at seventy, though his hair was pure silver and thinning at the temples.

"Glad to see you arrived safely," he said as he slid into the passenger seat of her Toyota. "How's life treating my favorite granddaughter?"

"Pretty good," Julie said, smiling and leaning across to kiss his cheek. "And how are you?"

"Fighting fit, I'm glad to say. And how are things at the *Philadelphia Star*?"

She made a wry face. "Much as usual. I had to practically go down on my knees to get this vacation, and then the editor could only let me have a few days because Marsha's off to London to cover the royal wedding. Her stuff will just about fill the Women's Page, but maybe I'll be allowed to do a few paragraphs about somebody's cute dog, or a new line in diapers."

John Elliott laughed. "You should have been a boy and come into the old firm."

"Grandpa," Julie said, giving him a mock frown, "if I'd wanted to study law, I'd have done it. My gender makes no difference."

"Whoops, sorry." Laughing to himself, he watched her snub-nosed profile and said fondly, "But I'm pretty glad you're a girl, Julie. You remind me of your grandma when she was young—or is that sexist talk, too?"

"I guess it's allowed. Anyhow, I never could resist your line of flattery. How come there aren't more men like you around today? They're all so dreary."

"All of them?" he asked in surprise.

"Well, all the ones I get to meet, anyway. Or is it something about *me* that's to blame?"

"Not from where I'm sitting," her grandfather assured her. "But I thought you were a career girl."

"So I am. But these days you can combine the two, can't you?"

"That depends. Do I detect a certain disenchantment with life?"

"Maybe it's the weather," Julie said. "Though sometimes it does all seem pretty futile. I get called into the office, told to go and cover a story, so I rush up to the library for cuttings and read them in the cab—I'm conscientious about doing my homework, in case you're interested. And when it's all done, what do I get from it? Maybe a couple of paragraphs without even a by-line, hidden under columns of stuff that Marsha's turned out."

"But when you called me last week, you were so excited!" John Elliott exclaimed. "That riot you covered . . ."

Julie's face brightened. "Oh, yes, that was something of a coup—I just happened to be in the right

9

place at the right time. It wasn't really a riot, just a demonstration outside a political meeting, but I did get interviews with the leaders. Hank Freeman seemed quite pleased. He actually smiled at me the next day. And there was quite a bit of favorable reaction. But since then, it's been back to routine."

"At least it was a start," he consoled her. "You're young yet. You'll go far. You're an Elliott."

Julie didn't argue, but she wondered if he knew that the family's constant harping on success was sometimes like a tightening chain around her throat. Maybe that was why she tended to put herself down— because they expected so much.

They arrived back at Red Oaks to be greeted with the news that there had been a phone call for Julie.

"Such a rude man!" her grandmother said, quivering with indignation. "He shouted at poor Helen, and then he shouted at me. I told him you were badly in need of this vacation, Julie, but he said—" She hesitated, her lips pursing in disapproval as she forced herself to repeat the phrase. "He said you were to get your butt back to the office if you know what's good for you."

"Sounds like Hank Freeman," Julie said, exchanging a glance with her grandfather. She was all too familiar with her editor's choice use of language when roused, but if her grandmother had quoted word for word, then Hank had been unusually restrained with her. "Did he say what it was about?"

"He did not," Mrs. Elliott replied. "When I asked him, he said that was his business, and if you valued your job, you'd do as you were told."

Shaking her head in sympathy, Julie said, "He's like that. He's not human when he's in a tailspin."

"Well, he can just wait," Mrs. Elliott declared, still ruffled with annoyance. "I told him I didn't know how long you would be gone, so there's no need to rush off at once. Besides, in this weather it will soon be dark, and you haven't eaten yet. Why not leave it until tomorrow? Maybe his temper will have cooled by then."

"He wouldn't call me back from vacation for no reason," Julie replied, wondering what on earth could have happened back at the office. "There was some talk that a congressman's wife had shown interest in that piece last week. Maybe she wants to give me an interview. I'd better call in and see."

"Use the extension in your room." Her grandmother sniffed. "And don't be long. It's nearly dinner time."

Hurrying up the stairs, Julie shut herself in her room and dialed the number of the *Philadelphia Star*, her imagination in top gear. Perhaps she was about to rise in the world, away from the Women's Page.

After a brief connection with the front desk, she found herself talking to Paul Collings, the assistant editor. "Hank's busy right now," he told her. "And I'm not saying a word. Just stop wasting time, Julie. Get back here fast. And, hey, drive safely. See you."

Whatever was causing the hurry, it seemed too intriguing to miss. With only a small regret for her interrupted vacation, Julie swiftly repacked her suitcase, said goodbye to her grandparents and Gary, and set out on the rain-swept road back to Philadelphia.

She drove straight to the *Philadelphia Star* building and walked into the familiar evening scene of chaos as the paper was prepared for the presses, whose subdued thunder already reverberated as the machinery was checked and oiled. People sat frowning over typewriters in a morass of papers and files; in a corner the teletype machine chattered to itself while boys ran between journalists and copyreaders carrying rewrites. Around the largest desk, Hank Freeman, Paul Collings, and a couple of others were bent over the rough proof of a page they were shaping for the first edition. As Julie appeared, the editor looked up, light glinting on his bronzed bald head. He caught her eye and yelled, "In my office! Wait there!"

Several people looked up from their work to exchange a word of greeting with her, and a dry voice commented, "Hi, Julie. Had a nice vacation?"

The walls of the editor's office were covered with awards and framed first pages bearing memorable headlines of the past. As Julie closed the door, the noise from the outer office lessened. She smelled the stale smoke that hung in the air. Hank's big desk was strewn with notes and memos whose significance only he knew, and heaven help anyone who moved one single sheet without his permission.

Fighting against the tense anticipation that was growing inside her, Julie perched on the edge of a chair by the door, certain now that her career was about to take an upswing. It must be the congressman's wife, probably so impressed by Julie's piece on the political demonstration that she had declared she would be interviewed only by the reporter who had written that copy—or so Julie's imagination decided.

Abruptly the door swung open, and Hank's massive figure marched in. He was built like a shambling bear, with his bald head always gleaming above steel-rimmed glasses that made his gray eyes look sharp. Striding to his chair, he threw himself down, leaned back, and squinted at her.

"You made good time," he conceded.

"It sounded urgent," Julie replied. "What's happened? Something to do with the Women's Page?"

"What else would it be? That's your department, isn't it?"

A sense of anticlimax swamped Julie like a dousing with muddy water. She was hungry, she was tired, she had driven well over two hundred miles that day, and her nerves were fraying. "You mean to say you took me away from my vacation for that? Paul made it sound as though it was important!"

"So it is. Important to our women readers."

Hank leaned forward suddenly, fixing her with one of his eagle stares, and for a moment she feared he might fire her for insolence. "Think I'm an ogre, do you?" he demanded. "Well, I'm about to prove that my heart is pure gold—fool's gold, maybe. You're still green, Julie, but you're learning. That piece you did last week was pretty fair journalism. So I'm going to give you a special assignment. Have you got a passport?"

The word sent her thoughts skittering haphazardly. "Why—yes. I got one last year, when I was due to take a trip to England, when my mother had that bad fall. Do you want me to go to Paris or something?"

"Or something," he agreed, throwing himself back in his chair and reaching for one of the thin black cigars he kept in his vest pocket. "Marsha's been taken sick. Appendicitis. She's been hospitalized and will have to undergo surgery. *That's* why I called you back. I want you ready to fly to London in a couple of days' time."

Julie stared at him, her face burning hot and then cooling as the shock hit her stomach, making it churn with excitement.

"Well?" Hank barked. "Can you handle the royal wedding?"

She swallowed hard. "Yes, sir, I surely can," she heard herself say and was glad that her voice sounded firm despite the butterflies in army boots leaping inside her.

Striking a match, Hank squinted at her through smoke. "For a moment I thought you were going to go all feminine on me. I'll be frank—if I had any choice I wouldn't be doing this, but as Marsha's number two, you have the right to give it a whirl. Young Tessa can fill in for you. What I want from you is details—every last thing you can dig up, and I warn you it won't be easy. The wedding gown, the cake, the bridesmaids —all the glamour you women go for. And if you can get interviews with anyone close to the bride and groom. . . ."

His eyes had narrowed as his newsman's instincts homed-in on the project, but he sighed and shook his head as if he realized he was asking the impossible. "Just do the best you can. Write something. Don't worry about hard news—I'll get that through the wire services. Just give me details, personal bits and pieces to fill out the picture. And if all else fails, enjoy yourself, because when you get back here, I'm going to work you so hard your feet won't touch the ground. Hell—I'm practically sending you on vacation after all."

Fully expecting to wake up and find she was day-dreaming again, Julie sat quite still, her head a maze of excited anticipation and whirling questions.

"You can arrange about traveler's checks tomorrow," Hank said. "Have you got an American Express card?"

"Yes, I have."

"Just remember not to go wild on your expenses. I'll count every cent when you get back. But come see the business office in the morning, and they'll fix up the finances. Got your notebook?"

It was in her hand in two seconds flat, her pencil poised to scribble.

"You'll report to me through Jim Dawes at International Press. Get the address from the office, but remember the name—Jim Dawes. Turn to him as you might turn to me." One of his rare smiles crossed his lips. "Only remember he won't want to pamper you. You'll be in over your head for a while, but you'll soon meet up with people. London will be crammed with reporters. Think you can cope?"

"I'm sure I can," she replied, cursing the croak in her voice.

His skeptical gaze seemed to doubt her competence. "You're all I've got, Julie, but I don't expect miracles. The world won't end if you don't come up with any exclusives. I don't think you really know what you're in for, though."

"Oh?" She stiffened her spine, ready to defend her professional ability, but the rueful glint in his eye worried her. "How do you mean, exactly?"

"It won't be anything like the States, I warn you," Hank informed her solemnly, pointing the glowing end of his cigar at her. "Here we're the Fourth Estate, and everyone accepts our right to get at the facts. Over there. . . . When you're dealing with the British royal family it's like nothing else on earth. They're close-mouthed—even their floor sweepers will clam up on you. You could probably get to interview President Reagan if you tried hard enough, but you won't get near the queen or her family—especially not the happy

14

couple, not at this time. Just be prepared to get doors slammed in your face if you overstep the lines they've drawn."

"I'm sure I'll manage, Mr. Freeman," Julie said stoutly, thinking that he must be exaggerating. There were always ways of getting information.

"Good." He rose from his chair, and she followed suit. "Now I've got a paper to put to bed, and from the looks of you, that's the place you ought to be. It's going to be a hectic two weeks for you. Oh, and one more thing. See the office about airline tickets and hotel bookings. They've got it all set." As he paused, he allowed himself another wry smile. "You're really in luck today. I happen to know that the chairman agreed that Marsha could pamper herself since she hates long flights. You'll be flying on the Concorde."

Two

Hank Freeman had said that after she got back he would work her so hard that her feet wouldn't touch the ground, but it seemed to Julie that she had been floating ever since he told her the news. Now she was really airborne, speeding across the Atlantic in supreme comfort, her eyes drawn every few minutes to the green-lit sign that informed passengers of their speed. Currently it read M:1.5—one and a half times the speed of sound. She almost had to pinch herself to believe it.

Beside her in the seat nearest the window, a businessman frowned over his files, occasionally stabbing a pad with a gold pen, making scribbled notes. Julie had tried to engage him in conversation; she had been bubbling over with excitement. But her bright remarks had drawn only monosyllabic answers, and she had soon given up. She had tried to read, but somehow her thoughts wouldn't stay on the book, and she had resorted to making a few notes of her own, jotting down her impressions of the flight as an introduction for her first article. New York to Heathrow, London, was less than a four-hour trip in the incredibly sleek white plane that flew so smoothly and silently, and a glance at her watch confirmed that they must already have entered the glide path.

Her heart was pounding uncomfortably fast, and only now did she admit to herself that mixed in with her excitement was a good leavening of apprehension. Not only was this the most important assignment she had yet been given, but it was the first time she had been outside the States, and she was completely on her own, without even the prospect of being met by a friendly face. She took care to maintain an outward appearance of nonchalance, but somewhere inside her those butterflies were stomping again.

"Ladies and gentlemen," came the cool British tones of the stewardess, "we shall be landing at Heathrow Airport in fifteen minutes, when local time will be nine p.m. Please fasten your seat belts and extinguish all cigarettes. We hope you have enjoyed your flight."

Calmly Julie reached for her seat belt and then had trouble getting it to click shut. Her palms were damp as she encountered the weary gaze of her neighbor.

"Here we go again," he said. "I only hope it doesn't take longer to get through customs than it did to cross the Atlantic."

Julie replied with an unsteady laugh, taking a deep breath as she leaned back in her seat and waited for the plane's wheels to contact English soil.

The landing was so easy that she was barely aware of it, and to her relief the deplaning process and passage through customs went with similar smoothness. Soon she was out in the main concourse, a heavy suitcase dragging on one hand and a bulky, many-pocketed bag, which she had carried on the plane as hand luggage, swinging from her shoulder. As in every airport throughout the world, the place was a bewildering mass of activity as people of many nationalities came and went. Somewhere a child cried, its screams piercing the noise of voices, rumbling luggage carts, and announcements from a loudspeaker. In the middle of it all Julie felt bewildered. A slim figure in a well-cut navy pants suit, her honey-gold hair

17

tumbling across one shoulder, she stood looking around for an exit sign.

To her surprise she realized that the distorted voice coming over the announcement system was saying her name: "Would Miss Julie Elliott please come to the enquiry desk? Miss Julie Elliott to the enquiry desk, please."

Turning around, she set off in the appropriate direction and was approaching the sign marked Enquiries when a tall, denim-clad man eased himself away from the wall and came striding toward her. "Are you Julie Elliott?"

"Why, yes," she replied in surprise. "What's wrong?"

"Nothing that I'm aware of." He looked her up and down, a dark eyebrow crooking slightly. "No wonder I couldn't pick you out. I expected some hard-faced old harridan."

Thoroughly disconcerted, Julie stared at him. "I beg your pardon?"

"No, I beg yours," he said. "Allow me to introduce myself. I'm Nick Tregarron. Jim Dawes asked me to come and meet you. He'd have been here himself, but there was some urgent conference he had to attend, and since we'll be working together, he thought we might as well get to know each other right away."

His deep-voiced English accent fascinated her so much that she failed to grasp the full significance of what he was saying.

"I'm not sure I understand. Working together? How do you mean?"

"I mean I've been delegated to do the photographs for you. It's not my usual line, but all Jim's staff photographers are busy, and since I owe him a favor, I said I'd do it."

"I see," Julie said blankly, though she didn't see at all. This man sounded less than pleased about the whole business, and she wondered just what kind of favor he owed Jim Dawes to make him undertake a commission he clearly didn't want.

"I've got my car outside," he said. "Shall we go? Oh—here, let me take that case, it looks heavy."

As he relieved her of the case, his fingers brushed hers, and she was aware of a scent of an herbal aftershave. He appeared to be in his early thirties, a tall, rangy man with broad shoulders filling out a denim jacket worn over a white shirt. Blue jeans covered long, long legs, and his dark hair curled around his ears and down his neck, but it was his air of unwillingness that intrigued her.

"I hadn't expected anyone to meet me," she said, struggling to keep up with his long strides. "I appreciate it."

"We couldn't let you fend for yourself, could we?" he replied. "You might have got lost or molested." But to judge by his tone of voice, that wouldn't have worried him in the least.

Very soon they were outside in the night air, where headlights glittered and illuminated the long lines of people waiting for taxis. Overhead the last faint smears of daylight were fading, though Julie's body clock told her it was only mid-afternoon. All the same she felt weary, thirsty, and horribly grubby, not to mention on edge because of the half-belligerent attitude of her companion.

"What did you say your name was?" she asked as she followed him toward a parking lot.

"Tregarron. Nick Tregarron." Without pausing in his stride he reached into his pocket and extracted a business card, which he held out for her to take. "You may as well have that, in case you need to get in touch with me."

A glance at the card showed her his name, his occupation, photographer, and an address and phone number. "Is this your office?"

"No, it's my home number. I work from home."

Keys jingled in his hand as he approached a white, open-topped, and gleaming MG which waited among rows of other vehicles. He unlocked the trunk and threw her case inside, then gestured her into the passenger seat.

What stopped her from climbing in she wasn't sure, except that she was in a strange country and his manner made her wary. She faced him across the car as he opened the driver's door.

"Can you prove that you know Jim Dawes?"

He paused, leaning on the door, his expression indistinct in the shadows of the parking lot. "I've given you my card."

"But it doesn't tell me anything. Forgive me, Mr. Tregarron, but I'd just like to be sure—"

"You think I'm a mugger? Or a rapist?" A heavy, irritable sigh escaped him. "Miss Elliott, how do you suggest I prove my trustworthiness? Perhaps you'd prefer to take a taxi. It's all the same to me. I've had a lousy day. I'm extremely tired. The last thing I needed was to drive out here at this hour, but I came because Jim Dawes asked me. All I want to do is get you safely installed in your hotel so that I can go home and get some sleep before we embark on this assignment. Would you like to call International Press? You might find someone there who knows me. Or perhaps you'd like to walk into town. Just make up your mind."

The weary indifference in his voice stung her, and without a word she slid into the comfortable red leather seat. Her escort threw himself in beside her, started the engine, then hesitated, both hands on the top of the wheel.

"You're right to be cautious, of course," he said in what might have been meant to be an apologetic tone. "You don't know me from Adam. But I assure you there isn't a dishonorable intention even in my subconscious, not right at this moment. Believe me?"

"I guess so," she said, though even then she wasn't entirely sure.

"Good. Then let's be off. The Delphinia, isn't it?"

As he backed out of the parking space, Julie recalled that she was actually in London, and the thought brought a thrill of heady excitement.

"Have you been to London before?" Nick Tregarron asked.

"I was supposed to be coming last year, but I had to call the trip off. My grandparents were over here a few years back, though, and one of my ancestors came from England."

"Oh yes? Whereabouts?"

"I'm not sure. Anyhow, I almost feel I'm coming home, in a way, though I never dreamed it would happen this way, not just when the royal wedding is taking place. I still have to pinch myself to believe it."

He glanced at her with a cynical smile. "Gets you like that, does it? All excited because of the romance of it all?"

"Of course!"

"Good grief!" he said under his breath. "I might have known it."

"Something wrong with that?" she demanded.

"No, no. But for heaven's sake don't keep going all dewy-eyed on me. It's bad enough having to take pictures of the whole damn charade without having you floating on pink clouds the whole time. We've got a job to do, Miss Elliott. Let's do it in a workmanlike manner."

Since she couldn't suddenly forget her joy at being involved with the wedding, she decided not to reply, though she did wonder why he should be so sour about it.

They were traveling along a multilane highway, with suburbs to either side. Chains of lights followed the lines of streets, and more light glowed behind curtained windows in houses and small apartment buildings. Everything seemed smaller than she had imagined, familiar and yet somehow alien, and as excitement surged through her anew she clutched her bulky bag on her lap, then tried to contain her flying hair as the cool night wind swept over them. The car headed ever deeper into the center of the haze of light that lit the sky ahead.

After a while they came off the highway onto a long suburban road that seemed to go on for miles, eventually running alongside a park.

"Kensington Gardens," Nick said above the roar of

the engine. "The Albert Memorial on your left, the Albert Hall on your right."

Those landmarks were soon followed by the expensive shopping area of Knightsbridge.

"Keep your eyes open," Nick said eventually. "You might see something you recognize."

Since she already had her eyes wide open, taking in everything in sight, the advice seemed unnecessary. To their left, another park lay in shadow, while to the right, a high, spiked wall hid whatever lay behind it. Then as the car reached another junction Julie saw a massive, white, floodlit monument ahead, crowned by gilded statues, with water running into a pool. It stood in the middle of a wide traffic circle with vehicles sweeping around it, and as the MG turned left with the flow, Julie was so busy staring up at the statue of a seated queen that she almost missed seeing the railings behind it, which guarded the front of a building that looked golden in the floodlights. Turning in her seat, she gazed behind at the rows of windows and the central balcony, scarcely believing her eyes.

"Buckingham Palace!"

"Go to the top of the class and give out pencils," Nick said dryly. "And this road we're on now is The Mall, where the wedding processions will drive in two weeks' time. Only two more weeks, thank heaven. It can't be over soon enough for me."

Ignoring his cynicism, Julie reveled in the sight of the wide, tree-lined avenue where white flagpoles stood ready, topped with gilded coronets and spear points. In two short weeks Lady Diana would be driving in the glass coach down this road to meet her bridegroom, with crowds cheering and waving on either side, bands playing, and mounted soldiers escorting her. She blushed easily, so it was said, but on that day her blushes would be disguised by a cloudy veil of white.

"I can hardly believe it!" Julie breathed almost to herself. "I'm really here. I'll see it with my own eyes."

"You'd probably see more if you stayed home and

watched it on television," Nick said. "London is going to be crammed to overflowing on that day. You won't be able to move for crowds, heaven help us."

"I won't care," she replied. "I'm here. That's all that matters."

"Even if it rains?"

"Even if it snows. Now that I'm here the weather can't get me down. Only two days ago I was depressed because it was raining in New Jersey. Can you imagine? Being in London is like a dream."

"Let's hope it doesn't turn into a nightmare, Cinderella," Nick said, giving her a sidelong smile. "Watch out. Trafalgar Square coming up."

They drove through an archway between huge, imposing buildings and emerged into a wide intersection, where to one side Nelson's column soared skyward, with bronze lions crouched by its base and fountains playing behind. A good deal of traffic obeyed the changing lights, but pedestrians wandered, enjoying the sights.

Very soon they came to the brightly lit streets around Soho, thronged with more crowds. In the convertible Julie felt the full effect: the aroma of hot dogs, the sound of voices, and the bustle of the place. Thousands of people seemed to be strolling about, in and out of restaurants and arcades, leaving theaters, and gambling with death among the traffic—all by the vivid light of neon signs. When the car stopped at traffic lights, the sheer mass of the crowds pressed in on all sides, laughter mingling with the hum of traffic, while big black taxis dodged in and out, their polished sides reflecting the gaudy light.

"There's Eros, see," Nick said, pointing to a statue set high above steps in the center of the intersection. Dark against the lights behind him, the winged boy stood perpetually tiptoe after releasing his arrow, and as they swept around him, Julie realized she was in Piccadilly Circus. She had seen it often in films, but nothing had prepared her for the thrill of actually being there.

Nick turned the car into a wide road lined with

bright shop windows, many of them showing celebratory displays for the royal wedding. Even on the lampposts, baskets full of flowers were hung, with flags of Britain fluttering above them.

"And that," Nick said, "is your introductory tour of London, Tregarron-style. I'd show you more, but I'm too tired, and I expect you'll be glad to get settled in at your hotel."

Actually she could have stood a lot more sightseeing from the windy comfort of his car, but now that he mentioned it she did feel ready for a bath and a meal of some kind, though London had made her adrenaline rise and driven away her tiredness. She felt so overwhelmed she hardly knew whether to laugh or cry.

Turning into a narrow side street, Nick eased the MG into a parking space and cut the engine, then turned to give her a slight smile. "Well, here we are."

"Where?" she asked.

A long forefinger drew her attention to a blue-lit sign further down the street, which read Delphinia Hotel. "For a journalist," he said dryly, "you're not very observant. Come on, let's get you booked in."

Despite her protests that she could manage, he insisted on carrying her suitcase as they walked down the street and climbed the few steps into a softly lit lobby, where display cases lined the paneled walls and a deep carpet felt soft beneath Julie's shoes. An elderly night porter appeared to help her sign in and give her a key, and she asked for sandwiches and coffee to be sent up to her room, with more coffee at seven-thirty the next morning and all the daily papers.

"All of them?" the porter queried.

"As many as you can find," she said. "I'm a reporter. I'm over here to cover the royal wedding."

He made some conventional reply, but she didn't hear it because she had just caught a glimpse of the expression on Nick Tregarron's face—a look that derided her ingenuous confidences.

"It's all right," he said when the porter would have taken Julie's suitcase. "We'll find the way. I shall be coming straight back down again, so you needn't worry. I've been delegated to take care of the young lady."

That was the second time he had used the word delegated, which implied some sort of pressure. As they rode up in the small elevator, Julie said, "You could have dropped me at the door. There was no need to trouble yourself."

"It was no trouble," he said.

"Liar," she responded, but he just gave her an unreadable look from eyes that she noticed were a deep velvet-brown; then the elevator stopped.

When they eventually found her room, he followed her inside and dumped her suitcase on the bed. The furnishings were all conventional, the decor in understated tones of brown and ocher, brightened by orange curtains and lampshade. An open door in the corner gave a glimpse of a darkened bathroom.

"It's a bit characterless," Nick said. "Still, hotels are all getting like that these days. Will you be all right?"

"Yes, thank you. I do appreciate your help, Mr. Tregarron. It was very kind of you to meet me."

"It was the least I could do," he replied, though the words were formal rather than sincerely meant. "Well, I'll probably see you tomorrow. Good night, Miss Elliott."

"Good night," Julie said, puzzled by his attitude.

As the door closed she became aware of the hum of a strange city around her. Nick had been right about the bland conformity of the room, and suddenly she felt very much alone, very aware of her youth and inexperience in this game she had been plunged into.

Putting aside the doubts, she kicked off her shoes and, giving a sigh of relief, went in stockinged feet to the window, where a thick net curtain hid the view. Beyond it she looked down two stories into the side street, with offices opposite and the blue neon hotel sign shedding light to her right. As she stood there, the MG drew away, coming past the hotel to disappear with a last flare of red taillights. With its leaving she

25

felt even more alone, knowing that tomorrow she would be faced with finding her way around a city of which she knew very little, chasing copy that every other journalist would be after.

Her fingers, nestling into her jacket pocket, came in contact with Nick's business card, and she took it out to read it again and make a note of the phone number. At least she did know one person in London now, even if he had turned out to be something of an enigma.

In an effort to restore her confidence, she took a warm shower and began to unpack but was interrupted by the arrival of a maid with the sandwiches and coffee she had ordered. The maid turned out to be an Italian who spoke little English, and when it came to giving a tip, Julie found herself staring in bewilderment at the few British coins she possessed, ending up by giving the girl a fifty-pence piece, which, to judge by her bright smile, was generous. Julie mused that it was obviously going to be the small things that would trip her unless she was careful.

Since she had brought plenty of background reading with her, she spent the remainder of the evening doing her homework and sketching out the framework of her build-up articles. A good deal of it would probably have to be a rehash of everything that had been written already, since she had little hope of getting interviews with any of the people most closely concerned, but she comforted herself that Hank Freeman had said he didn't expect any scoops, which was probably just as well. The more she thought about the actual job ahead of her, the less confident she felt.

Sleep seemed a long time coming. Her head was full of plans and dreams, but when eventually she did succumb, there appeared to be no transition before there was a knock on the door, followed by the click of a key as another maid brought morning coffee—and a dismaying mass of newsprint. All the morning newspapers.

As Julie struggled to sit up, she felt like death, as if it were still the middle of the night. The coffee proved to be a lifesaver, but her brain remained fuddled as she thumbed through the newspapers in search of any stories that might give her a lead.

Feeling a need to look bright and efficient, even if she didn't feel it, she took a shower and chose to wear red and white—white slacks, red shirt, and a spotted scarf knotted loosely round her throat. A comb soon dealt with her hair, but her face looked pale, and the green eyes that stared back at her from the mirror were full of uncertainty. Had she really believed she could handle this assignment as well as Marsha Harris could have done? Was she enough of a professional? Yes, of course she was, she told herself firmly, but saying it and believing it were two different things.

She took her time eating a full English breakfast, hoping it would help to wake her up, but she still felt edgy as she went to the reception desk, cashed a traveler's check, then asked the girl if she would call a taxi.

The sky was overcast, with a few spots of rain in the wind. Luckily she had grabbed a waterproof jacket before she left her room. She put it on as she waited on the hotel steps. To her delight, one of the big black London taxis drew up, the driver leaning out to inquire if she was the lady who had sent for him. She gave him the address of International Press and climbed into the roomy interior of the car.

"This your first time in London, is it, love?" the cabbie asked through the open window between them.

"Yes, it is," Julie admitted.

"Is it like you expected?"

She looked out at the traffic that choked the road they had turned into—cars, trucks, and huge red double-decker buses, which towered over them like leviathans—and laughed. "Not exactly. I had visions of creeping fog, and men all wearing striped trousers and bowler hats."

"Oh, you'll see some of them around," the driver said. "As for the fog—you've been watching too many old movies. I haven't seen an old-fashioned pea-souper in years."

As he drove he gave her a running commentary on

27

places of interest, so she was constantly craning out of one window or another to look at buildings whose stone shone near-white, at statues and fountains, and the lush greenery of trees and grass in parks and the little squares that dotted London. On all sides, she could see evidence of history, and it felt strange to be where kings and queens had once ridden, as if her school history books might come to life at any moment.

Then they were in Fleet Street, and the cabbie drew her attention to the offices of famous newspapers before he turned down a narrow side road and stopped.

"Here we are then, love. International Press. A journalist, are you?"

"Yes. I'll be covering the royal wedding."

"Lucky old you," he said, grinning. "It's going to be a wonderful day. Good old Charlie, Gawd bless 'im. Gawd bless both of 'em, I say. I'll be drinking their health, unless I'm working. Maybe even if I am working." He gave her a broad wink and informed her of the price of the ride, so she paid him and added a generous tip, pleased by his friendliness.

The offices of International Press were housed in a tall narrow building crammed shoulder to shoulder with others of similar size. A couple of steps led up to a brass-plated door, and beyond lay an entrance lobby where a bespectacled girl sat behind a desk. Trying to conceal the fact that she was almost shaking with nerves, Julie gave the girl her name and asked to see Jim Dawes.

"Oh, yes, Miss Elliott, he's expecting you," the girl said, giving Julie a smile and a quick glance that sought to sum her up. "Up the stairs, first door on your left. Just knock and go in."

Julie's low-heeled shoes sounded loud on metal-edged treads and a corridor floored with linoleum. As she reached the door she paused to straighten her shoulders, toss back her hair, and clear her throat before knocking—rather harder than she had intended.

It was a small office, cramped with filing cabinets, a

couple of chairs, an old wooden fireplace painted a
uniform gray with the walls, and a large cluttered desk
behind which sat a thin, wiry man with a shock of gray
hair that looked as if it had never seen a comb. He
glanced up, did a double take, and said, "Yes?"

"Are you Mr. Dawes?" she inquired. "I'm Julie
Elliott."

"You're—" He stopped himself, but he couldn't hide
his dismay, and she knew without having to be told
that he thought her much too young to handle the
assignment. Which meant that she must take care to
prove him wrong. She must be tough and self-confi-
dent and not tell him, as she had hoped to tell him, that
on her first day she was feeling like a fish that had
taken a spirited leap for pure joy of living and found
itself floundering on dry land, half dazed.

He got to his feet, holding out his hand, which she
shook across the desk, trying to hide her surprise at
his stature—he was little over five feet tall.

"Welcome to London, Julie," he said, avoiding her
eyes. "Sit yourself down." His gesture led her into a
hard, straight-backed chair that did not encourage
long visits, and she could see from his expression that
he still had doubts about her.

"You've, er, got settled in okay, have you?" he asked.
"Hotel all right for you? Good. I understand Nick
Tregarron was able to meet you after all. I rang him up
late last night to check, after I got back from my
conference. If it hadn't been for that, I'd have met you
myself. Hank said I was to take care of you." Pausing,
he let his glance flick over her again and frowned. "He
didn't tell me you were so young, though."

"He wouldn't have sent me if he hadn't thought I was
competent," Julie said.

"No, maybe not," he replied dubiously. "And to tell
you the truth, I've got enough on my hands at the
moment, so I'll just brief you about the setup here and
let you get on with it. Hank said he'd given you a free
hand."

"That's right," she said, her confidence ebbing even

further because he was telling her, in the nicest possible way, that he didn't want to be pestered with her problems.

He informed her that there was a reporters' room where she might type up her copy, which had to be ready by nine o'clock, at the latest, on the evening prior to publication. Preferably earlier, to save wear and tear on his nerves. The office would provide anything she might need in the way of press handouts or research material, and once she had completed her final drafts, his staff would wire them to Philadelphia for her.

"I don't think there's much of interest for you today," he added, sorting through some papers on his desk. "The queen's due to open the Humber Bridge tomorrow, but that won't affect you. Do you expect to have any copy for us today?"

"No," she said. "My buildup articles will be run from Monday and today's . . . what is it, Thursday? But I'm planning to work a day or two ahead, to allow for any hitches—or last-minute newsbreaks. I'll try to get Monday's copy ready for you tomorrow, then you can wire it at your convenience."

She at last saw a hint of grudging approval in his face as he laced his hands together and stared at her across them. "Maybe old Hank's not as soft as I thought," he said, then reached out to grab the phone as it began to ring. "Yes? . . . Oh, fine, she'll be down right away. Thank you." As he replaced the receiver he glanced at Julie. "Nick Tregarron has arrived. He'll see you through, though this isn't his usual line. But Nick's the best. He'll do okay for you. Well, good luck, Julie."

He pushed his slight frame from the chair once more, shook her hand, and went back to his work as if relieved to have got over one more hurdle in his busy day. None of it was calculated to make her feel any better.

As she went down the stairs she saw her reluctant photographer draped half across the desk chatting to the receptionist, who was laughing up at him in obvious delight. She glanced at Julie, and Nick swung around, the smile fading from his face as his glance flicked from her hair to her shoes in quick assessment.

That morning he was wearing a rainproof jacket with his jeans, and from one broad shoulder swung a metal equipment case. Regarding him through narrowed eyes, Julie wondered if it was only the assignment he didn't relish or whether he had taken a personal dislike to her. Perhaps he, too, thought her too young to deal with the job she had been given.

"Good morning, Miss Elliott," he greeted with no discernible expression.

"Good morning," she returned coolly, suddenly feeling irritated. Her head seemed to be full of cotton candy.

"Well, are we ready?" Nick said. "Shall we go?"

"By all means." Stalking past with head high, she went out to the sidewalk, pausing to breathe deeply of the humid air. She was depressingly aware that she had no idea where to begin her assignment, and the thought of having Nick Tregarron as a witness to her floundering made the situation worse.

Behind her, Nick emerged from the building with languid strides. "Where are we heading?"

"We'll take a cab," she said, thinking that would give her a few minutes to come up with a bright idea.

"Oh, no, we won't," he argued at once. "Cabs are expensive. Everything you might want to see is within walking distance. Everybody walks in London. It's the only way to get to know the city properly. I'm glad to see you've got sensible shoes on, even if those white slacks are going to be filthy before we're done. Where do you want to go?"

Exasperated by his gall in criticizing her clothes, she flung her arms out. "I don't know!"

"You want me to decide for you? Okay, we'll go this way. And one of the first things you'll have to do is buy a detailed street map."

Without waiting for a reply he strode off, and she was obliged to hurry after him, biting her lip against a desire to ask him to walk more slowly.

They came out into Fleet Street, and despite her still

fuzzy head she was aware of a certain thrill at being in the mecca of the newspaper world. The street hummed with traffic, and pedestrians crammed the sidewalks in front of shops, cafés, and pubs, which had not yet opened. But what interested Julie most were the vast buildings housing world-famous newspaper offices. Had she been in different company she might have expressed her excitement, but with Nick Tregarron as a companion, she clamped her teeth against exclamations of touristlike joy.

Outside a stationery store Nick stopped, nodding at the door. "Here's where you buy your map. Got any British currency?"

"Of course I have," Julie said shortly.

She soon purchased the map and was unable to resist buying two royal wedding souvenir pencils plus a key ring, the fob of which bore portraits of the happy couple. But when she returned to the street, her pleasure in these small purchases evaporated in face of Nick's sardonic look.

"Pencils I'll need," she said defensively. "And I collect key rings."

"If you say so," he replied. "But if you ask me, this wedding business has got out of hand. It's turning into one great commercial merry-go-round."

"Not to the two people most closely involved, it's not!"

Nick snorted in disgust. "I forgot you were starry-eyed about it all. Good grief, everybody's tightening belts, there are millions out of work, and just because one couple is taking the plunge—"

"They're not just any couple, are they?" Julie interrupted. "He's the Prince of Wales—your future king."

"Yes, and if he had his way he'd probably prefer to slip quietly away to some country church and do without all the hoo-hah. I wouldn't be in his shoes for a fortune."

She stared at him coldly, absently noting the way the sun glinted russet on his hair as the clouds momentarily parted, though its attraction was diminished by the angry look on his face.

"If you feel that way, why did you ever take this assignment?" she demanded.

"Because I have a living to earn. I was planning to be out and about with my camera anyway, for a book I'm doing."

"What sort of book?"

"I've been commissioned to make a visual record of the wedding summer."

This calm announcement almost robbed her of words. "When you hate the very idea of it all? How *can* you?"

"Because it's too good a free show to miss. But don't run away with the idea that I'm interested in the romantic angle. I'm not. What I intend to record is the wedding's effect on ordinary people—the offbeat slant."

"Seen through jaundiced eyes," Julie said darkly.

A wry smile caused a dimple to form in one of his cheeks as he swung back into his stride, a hand beneath her elbow to guide her across a busy intersection, beneath a railway bridge, and up a sloping street. Anger and stubborn pride prevented her from asking where they were going, so she took little notice of her surroundings and was amazed when they rounded a final corner and came face to face with an edifice with wide steps, and pillars and porticoes that lifted skyward.

"I thought you'd want to see the place where His Royal Highness is going to say goodbye to his freedom," Nick said. "There it is—Saint Paul's Cathedral."

Three

The entrance to the cathedral was already adorned with scaffolding for TV cameras that would relay pictures of the wedding around the world. A renewed sense of awe filled Julie as she and Nick climbed the steps to enter the cool, hushed atmosphere of Saint Paul's, where hundreds of wandering tourists dwindled into insignificance beside the soaring symmetry of Christopher Wren's architecture.

In this part of the cathedral color was subdued, with only bare natural tones. Plain wooden chairs stood in rows on a floor of checkered black and white marble. Even the windows were of plain frosted glass, while at regular intervals along the aisle, polished brass gratings in the floor gave glimpses of the functional rooms below.

Lady Diana in her bridal gown would walk down this aisle, Julie thought. The marble was slippery, and the holes in the brasswork might prove dangerous to high heels. But when she remarked on the fact Nick informed her sardonically that naturally there would be a red carpet laid on the great day.

The hum of voices seemed lost in the spaces below the vaulted ceiling, and on either side fluted pillars soared to archways above white marble statues. A group of schoolchildren straggled by, accompanied by a guide, and then as Julie followed the bridal path, she became aware of the great dome above. For a while she stood awestruck, gazing up into the lofty painted spaces of the dome. Far above, people were looking down over the gilded balustrade of the Whispering Gallery. Batteries of lights hung ready to illuminate the scene for the television audience.

A wooden dais had been erected in front of the choir, and beyond it the cathedral exploded with color. Glittering gold of paintings dazzled the eye, and light caught in glass mosaics brilliant with color, while below was the dark magnificence of carved wood that formed the choir. Tall-stemmed lights with orange shades would illuminate the choristers' music, and beyond was the high altar itself, framed by twisted and gilded pillars and backed by the rainbow colors of a stained-glass window.

Listening to one of the guides, who was speaking to a group of visitors, Julie took rapid notes, recording the man's words and her own impressions. For a few moments she actually forgot her tiredness in the wonder of her surroundings.

Approaching one of the black-cassocked church officials, she questioned him about the wedding and was delighted when he informed her that the window behind the high altar belonged to the American Memorial Chapel. "Dedicated to your fellow countrymen who died over here during the war," he added.

That same window would shed its colored light over Prince Charles and Lady Diana, Julie thought, a lump in her throat. It was a detail her readers would love.

She glanced around for Nick but, unable to see him at that moment, decided she would find him later. She paid the entrance fee to go into the ambulatory beside the choir and then to the American Memorial Chapel. It was a splendor of gilded wooden panels and black wrought-iron screens protecting the small altar, with the spectacular window towering over it. The Book of Remembrance lay open in a glass case, and Julie glanced at the names there, wondering if her Uncle

Richard was recorded on one of the pages. Suddenly she was impatient to have pictures.

Nick Tregarron, she thought, was going to be a fine helper if he disappeared every time she needed him. Suddenly all her tiredness and ill temper flooded back as she set out to find him, walking rapidly back into the main body of the building, where tourists were staring around the cathedral.

Eventually, breathless and irritated, she found Nick in one of the side aisles taking shots of people who were paying two pounds to have their name printed on a document thanking them for their donation. Buy Two Minutes of History read the signs.

"For heaven's sake!" She sighed. "I've been looking for you for ages."

Busy taking one final picture, he ignored her until it was done, then he put away his camera and said, "I told you I'd meet you by the crypt entrance in ten minutes. It was you who didn't turn up."

"When did you say that?"

"You were gazing up into the dome at the time."

"Oh, really! I didn't hear you. I was miles away."

"But you answered me," he informed her. "I suppose you were too busy dreaming to take much notice— thinking about standing there beside your own Prince Charming, I expect."

His sarcasm was overlaid by a spark of real annoyance, but she was too angry to take heed of it. "Whatever I was doing, you're supposed to be here to help me. How can we work together if you're going to vanish half the time?"

"I didn't vanish. I thought you'd taken in what I said. It was a misunderstanding, but then you're determined to misunderstand me, aren't you, Julie? So what is it you want me to do?"

"I need some pictures of the American Memorial Chapel—particularly the window. And general shots of the cathedral."

"Those I've done," he informed her shortly. "Okay, I'll go and get the rest. Why don't you sit down and rest your legs?"

Clearly he didn't want her with him, and since he knew more about taking photographs than she did, she left him to it and wandered to a chair near the choir, where she sat wishing she didn't feel so washed out.

After a while Nick reappeared, said he had taken a good selection of pictures, and was sure one or two of them would be suitable for her purposes. "Now if you've done all you want to do here, perhaps we ought to move on."

"That suits me fine," Julie said, but this time when he strode ahead, she didn't bother to try and keep up with him. He was a completely exasperating man, and she had begun to blame him for all her troubles, though she knew that was irrational.

She paused for a while on the great pillared porch of the cathedral, in front of iron-studded doors that towered behind her as she drank in the view that would greet the bride and groom after they were married. Hopefully they would emerge into sunlight to stand at the top of the steps while a thousand cameras whirred and clicked, bells peeled, and crowds cheered. But for Julie the sunlight was hazy, no bells rang, and on the road only the constant stream of traffic rushed up and down Ludgate Hill. However, she promised herself that she would be somewhere in that cheering crowd when the day arrived, and hopefully her press pass would make it possible to get near the cathedral.

When eventually she came out of her daydreams and made her way down the wide steps, she found Nick waiting beside the statue of Queen Anne, who was staring down Ludgate Hill, apparently trying to direct the traffic with her scepter.

"It's about time we had some lunch," Nick said, glancing at his watch. "If we go now we'll miss the main rush."

"Whatever you say," Julie replied indifferently, though the thought of a meal and a drink—not to mention a rest—was appealing. "Where do you suggest?"

He pretended astonishment. "Are you asking my

advice? We could try the Cheshire Cheese, if you like. It's worth a visit, if you're interested in quaint old historical places. They say Samuel Johnson often used to go there."

"It sounds fine," Julie said. "Where do we go?"

"Back the way we came. It's off Fleet Street."

To prove that she did have some sense of direction, she marched away, pausing at the curb to glance left for traffic. She had begun to step into the road when a rough hand grabbed her and pulled her back. She found herself wrapped firmly in Nick's arms, protesting at his brutality in the moment before she registered the presence of a huge red bus that blasted past on a wave of dust and diesel fumes. It had come, of course, from the right.

"Idiot!" Nick exclaimed, brown eyes flashing fury at her. "If you can't remember which side we drive on, at least look both ways."

"There was no call to be so rough!" she returned, shaken by the near accident as she pushed him away and rubbed her arm where his fingers had bruised her. "I'll be black and blue tomorrow."

"I suppose you would have preferred to be squashed flat!"

For a moment they stood glaring at each other, spots of color burning on Julie's cheeks; then she turned away and this time made sure the road was clear in both directions before she walked across, with Nick at her heels. He remained a pace behind her right shoulder as she marched on, back down the busy Ludgate Hill and into Fleet Street, where she congratulated herself that at least there was one small part of the city that was now familiar to her.

"Now where?" she asked, not looking at her companion.

"Just across the road. You can't miss the sign. There's a narrow passageway into a courtyard—if you don't mind eating alone in a pub."

Dismayed, she turned to face him. "I thought you were coming with me."

His face was impassive, but his eyes glinted as he

said flatly, "That was the general idea, but I thought perhaps you'd sooner be alone. Let's face it, Miss Elliott, we're like oil and water. So unless there are any more pictures you might need today, I may as well relieve you of my presence."

What on earth did he mean? she wondered. Of course she wanted him to stay. She hated to eat alone, especially in strange places. Did he really mean to leave her stranded?

"Unless . . ." Nick said quietly, "you'd like me to stick around."

Tossing her hair back, she said carelessly, "You can do as you please. Don't feel responsible for *me*, Mr. Tregarron. I'm able to take care of myself."

A dark eyebrow raised derisively. "Yes, I must say you've demonstrated that quite adequately. Left to your own devices you'd probably by now be lost—or in hospital after walking under a bus. You're too damn stubborn for your own good. Oh . . ." he sighed heavily, taking her arm to guide her across the road. "We've both got to eat. We may as well do it together. But will you try not to keep biting my head off every time I open my mouth?"

"I will if you'll stop being so patronizing," she retorted, then allowed herself to be propelled between two stationary cars and through a stream of immobile traffic to the far sidewalk, where she saw the passageway he had described.

The place lay in deep shadow, one of the quiet corners that abound in London, as Julie was to discover. Ahead, the misty sun lit a corner of a towering office block, but in the narrow passageway little, dark old buildings huddled. Julie saw the open doorway of the Old Cheshire Cheese, its step so bowed under the weight of time that an iron grille had been set to protect it. It led into a narrow lobby, with sawdust on the floor and a twisting wooden stair leading to upper stories. To the left was a small dining room, while to the right was a little bar, patronized by only a few people.

Julie felt as though she had stepped into the past,

for the room remained basically unchanged after three hundred years of use: dark wooden walls and ceiling, old paintings—including one of the writer Samuel Johnson, whose local pub this had been—an open fireplace now black and empty, scrubbed tables and hard benches, and a bare floor strewn with more sawdust. Only the bar accoutrements and the friendly barmaids were of the 1980s.

"Hey, Nick!" a voice cried, and a young man leaped up from a bench. "I haven't seen you in ages. Where've you been hiding?"

"I've been around," Nick said warily. "Oh, Hal Greaves —Julie Elliott."

The young man turned his smile on her, shaking her hand warmly. He was slim and very fair, with bright blue eyes that paid compliments. "Hello, Julie, glad to meet you. Boy, but Nick has good taste. He always could pick the winners. Can I buy you a drink?"

"I'd love one," Julie said, moistening her dry lips. "A grapefruit juice, please."

"Is that all? Nothing stronger?"

"Not at this time of day, thanks."

Hal Greaves's eyes narrowed, though he was still smiling. "You're American," he observed. "Where did he find you? *I* never run into women like you."

"We're working together," Nick said. "And if you're buying, Hal, mine's a pint."

Aware that she was sticky and disheveled, Julie excused herself and made her way up several flights of wooden stairs, past other eating rooms and kitchens from which appetizing aromas floated. The whole building was made of wood, a tall and narrow place painted dark brown.

She splashed water on her face in a futile effort to wake herself up, then drew a comb through her windswept hair, telling herself that she ought to try being a little more friendly. Fate had decreed that she and Nick must work together, even if they were, as he had said, like oil and water.

Accordingly, she returned to the dark little bar with a smile ready to be tacked into place when needed. She found it easier to be relaxed with the humorous Hal Greaves around. His flirting came as a relief after Nick's aloofness.

Hal seemed to have invited himself to lunch, so they moved into the Chop Room where they sat at bare wooden tables on hard, high-backed benches and ordered. It was Hal who did most of the talking, in an amusing way that had Julie responding despite her mind's tendency to wander. She felt as though she hadn't slept for days.

Hal apparently owned a souvenir shop in the West End and had been in the pub to meet a business acquaintance who had not turned up.

"Still," he said unconcernedly, "you can't win 'em all. So you two are working together, eh? Sounds intriguing. I thought you preferred to work on your own, Nick. Or is she your model?"

"Hardly," Nick replied, giving Julie a bleak glance. "I'm just helping Miss Elliott out. She's over here to cover the wedding, and I've been roped in to take pictures for her."

"So you're a journalist?" Hal inquired, his eyes alight with interest.

Encouraged, Julie began to talk about her work and her excitement when she had been given this big assignment. Hal asked intelligent questions and seemed fascinated by every word she spoke, but each time she glanced at the silent Nick she caught him with one corner of his mouth awry.

"If you only arrived last night," Hal said eventually, "you won't have had time to see the sights. I'm not doing anything special this afternoon. How about letting me play guide? Or had you got something else planned?"

He glanced for answer at Nick, who shrugged eloquently and said, "I've got my own work to do. And I'd better be getting on with it. I'll just get the bill." Catching the waitress's eye, he beckoned her over.

"I'll pay for the meal," Julie offered. "I'm on an expense account."

Nick fixed her with a dark look that told her to be

quiet, counted some notes from his wallet, and got to his feet. "Well, I'll be seeing you," he said. "You know where to get in touch with me if you need me."

"Yes, but—" She stopped as he leaned on the table, looking her in the eye, saying meaningfully, "And you should smile more often. It suits you."

Before she could figure out what that meant, he had gone, leaving her perplexed, and newly annoyed with him. It was typical of him to disappear just when she was relying on him.

"If you've finished," Hal said, "shall we go? We could do the Tower, or take a trip on the river. Whatever you fancy."

"Let's get out of here first," she replied.

When she emerged from the passageway into Fleet Street, there was no sign of Nick in either direction, and she had the odd feeling that she had chased him away by being too friendly with Hal Greaves. Hal was pleasant enough, personable and amusing, but somehow the thought of spending the afternoon trailing round London with him was not appealing. What she really wanted to do, she realized, was to sleep.

"Where is it to be, then?" he asked, smiling. "The Tower, the river, Hyde Park? Though by the look of those clouds, we might do better visiting a museum."

"I'm afraid I wouldn't be much company," she said apologetically. "I'm sorry, Hal. I don't know what's wrong with me. I woke up feeling tired, and it's just getting worse."

"It's jet lag," he said at once. "It gets some people that way. Best thing you can do is sleep it off. But you're not getting away that easily. If you won't come sightseeing, how about letting me take you to the theater? Say tomorrow night. You should feel better by then."

She felt she ought to refuse but, being too exhausted to think of any good excuse on the spur of the moment, said lamely, "Well . . . yes, thank you."

"Where are you staying?" Hal asked. "I'll call you to make arrangements after I've got the tickets."

She gave him the name of her hotel, and then he stepped into the road to flag down a passing taxi for her, helping her into it and giving her a final smile. "'Bye, Julie. See you tomorrow."

Back at the Hotel Delphinia, Julie slept for the rest of the afternoon and woke in time to watch an early evening TV show from Caernarvon Castle, concerning Prince Charles and his role as Prince of Wales. After having dinner in the hotel restaurant, she returned to her room intending to do some more background reading, but soon her eyelids drooped again, and, astounded by her own tiredness, she settled down and knew no more until the maid arrived in the morning with her coffee and another armful of newspapers.

On that day her morning shower really woke her up. She felt bright, energetic, and full of enthusiasm for the task ahead. Too late, she realized that she should have given herself a day to get used to the time change before plunging into the assignment. Her memories of the previous day were all blurred, except that she was sure she had been horribly testy with Nick Tregarron. On reflection, he seemed to have been as helpful as was possible—though of course he had done it in his own offhand way.

One consolation was that her notes on Saint Paul's had been comprehensive and she had the material for her first article. After breakfast she consulted her map for the best route to Fleet Street, and it was only then that she realized how circuitous a route Nick had taken that first evening to give her an "introductory tour of London, Tregarron-style," even though he had been tired. So in spite of his apparent disinterest he had actually gone out of his way to please her. She was going to have to do some sincere apologizing.

In the busy reporters' room at International Press, she spent most of the morning typing and refining her article and making friends with other overseas correspondents. The place had a bustling air that made her feel at home, but every time the door opened, she glanced up hoping to see Nick Tregarron arrive. As the time passed and he did not appear, she began to feel

43

even worse about her behavior the previous day. After all, he was doing her a favor by taking pictures for her when he had his own book to think about.

Eventually, leaving the final draft of her article for wiring later that day, she went along to Jim Dawes's office intending to ask exactly what arrangements he had made with Nick, but to judge from the sound of voices beyond the door, the bureau chief was in heated conference. Deciding not to interrupt him, Julie turned away and went down the stairs to the lobby, where the red-haired receptionist looked up brightly from behind her desk.

"How's it going?" she asked.

"Oh, fine, thanks," Julie replied, searching her memory for the girl's name, which she had heard during the morning. Oh, yes—it was Maddie Venables. "I think I'm beginning to find my feet at last."

"Rather you than me," Maddie said, pushing her large, blue-rimmed spectacles further up her nose. "I couldn't do your job. I'd be hopeless in a foreign country. I wouldn't know where to start."

"To be honest, I feel kind of lost myself," Julie admitted. "This is the most important assignment I've ever been given, but it's different from anything I've done before."

"I suppose it would be," came the reply, accompanied by a sympathetic look that vanished in a grin. "Still, at least you've got Nick Tregarron as compensation. He's gorgeous, isn't he?"

"I can't say I'd noticed," Julie said, lying. "He hasn't been in today, has he?"

"Oh, yes, first thing this morning."

"What? But didn't he wait?"

"He just looked in to bring some pictures. Of Saint Paul's, I think he said. But he wasn't here long, and he didn't say if he'd be coming back. Pity. A visit from him quite makes my day."

The dreamy look on the pert face behind those huge glasses made Julie smile a little wryly. "He obviously turns on the charm with you."

"Oh, I think it's just his way," Maddie said. "Natural charm, if you know what I mean. Some men have it, some don't. Anyhow, I'm not stupid enough to take him seriously. I know he's not likely to look twice at me, not in that way—not when he's practically engaged to a raving beauty of an actress."

For some reason the news struck Julie like a blow in the ribs. "Is he?"

"So Mr. Dawes told me. He caught me drooling one day and said I was barking up the wrong tree. Still, there's plenty more fish in the sea, as they say. But I'd better get on before someone comes and catches me gossiping. Nice talking to you, Julie. Oh, by the way . . . if you ever feel lost and need someone to talk to, you can always ring me. I'm in the phone directory. The address is Hampstead."

"Thanks, I'll remember that," Julie said.

As she came out into the narrow street, she wondered about the sudden hollow space inside her. She had assumed that Nick Tregarron was unattached, but now that she thought about it, that was ridiculous. A man like Nick would naturally have a woman somewhere in his life. But if he was so endowed with "natural charm," how come he had been sour with her from the moment they met?

Feeling oddly restless, she walked by the river, where pleasure boats and barges plied the broad Thames. Swift clouds chased in a brisk breeze, occasionally tossing down a shower that Julie ignored as she found her way, by the landmark of Big Ben's clock face, to the Houses of Parliament and from there to the bustle of the square beyond, with Westminster Abbey standing impervious to the seething mass of people and rushing traffic. After the jostling on crowded pavements, she came thankfully to the cool green spaces of a park, where people strolled and ducks swam in greedy flotillas across a lake, crowding and quarreling at the places where children threw crumbs. She took the opportunity to pause and chat about the wedding, adding to her store of quotes from Londoners and visitors alike, since she planned to write about the mood of joyous anticipation that underlaid the everyday life of the city.

It was late afternoon before she returned to the Delphinia, to be told that a gentleman had called several times that day to speak to her. Despite herself, her spirits lifted at the thought that Nick had not forgotten her.

"Did he leave a message?" she asked.

The receptionist glanced at the piece of paper beside her. "He said he'd pick you up about seven o'clock."

"He did? But . . . was that all he said?"

"It was. He seemed to think you would know what it meant. But if there's some doubt, perhaps you should ring him and make sure. It was a Mr. Greaves. Hal Greaves, so he said."

Julie tried to conceal her disappointment, but her voice was flat as she spoke her thanks and collected her key. Until that moment she had completely forgotten agreeing to go to the theater with Hal, and now she wished she had done no such thing.

Half intending to phone him and call off the date, she went to her room and consulted the appropriate section of the weighty telephone directory, only to be confronted by so many Greaveses that she sighed and gave up, not knowing Hal's address. Anyway, a night out might cheer her up. At least she wouldn't sit around hoping that Nick might call.

Since she had plenty of time before Hal would arrive, she treated herself to a cool bath and shampoo, during the course of which it struck her that since she was supposed to be working with Nick, there was no reason why *she* shouldn't call *him*. She had seen no sign of him all day, nor had he tried to contact her, even when he had called in at the IP office.

Sitting wrapped in towels, she dialed his number, listened to it purr as it rang, and wondered if he was still out somewhere. She was about to put down the receiver when the purring stopped. The voice that answered was disconcertingly female. "Hello? Yes?"

"Is this—" Julie said uncertainly, "Mr. Tregarron's number?"

"Yes, it is. Did you want to speak to Nick? I'm afraid he isn't here at the moment. May I take a message?"

"Oh—no, thank you. It's not important," Julie said, her mind gone blank with shock. "I'll try again later."

"Just as you like, though I'm not sure what time he'll be home this evening. May I tell him who called?"

"My . . . my name's Julie Elliott," she faltered, then felt obliged to explain, "I'm a reporter. Nick's been taking pictures for me."

"Oh, yes, Miss Elliott," the voice replied. "He told me about that. I'll tell him you called. Perhaps he'll ring you back when he gets in."

"Fine," Julie said.

Even after she had hung up, that voice haunted her. It has sounded very cool, very English, and very much at home. Julie told herself that today it was perfectly okay for couples to live together, though that state was still called by various euphemisms. "Practically engaged," as Maddie Venables had put it, was as good a way of expressing it as any, and there was really no good reason why this confirmation of Nick's private way of life should make her feel personally insulted.

In an effort to restore her flagging morale, she took great care over her appearance that evening and determined to enjoy her evening at the theater with Hal Greaves. She fastened her hair up in an elegant style and put on a silky green dress with matching high-heeled sandals and a lacy white shawl, but all the time she kept catching herself wishing that her escort could have been Nick Tregarron and not his fair-haired friend. Which was not sensible. She rationalized that she hardly knew Nick, but her feelings were not responding to logic, unfortunately. She kept remembering a few brief seconds when she had been locked in Nick's strong arms, close enough to sense the muscular warmth of his body and the clean odor that hung around him. The memory disturbed her.

When, eventually, she stepped out of the elevator

into the hotel lobby, Hal Greaves came to greet her with a smile. He, too, had gone to some trouble with his grooming, wearing a velvet suit in midnight blue, but he wasn't as tall as Nick and his hair was straight and fair as Apollo's, not curled and dark with russet lights. Even blue eyes full of admiration found no favor with Julie that night, since she seemed to have developed a preference for eyes of a dark brown—enigmatic eyes that chided and mocked. Oh, pull yourself together! she chided herself inwardly, outwardly finding a smile for the presentable young man whom, in other circumstances, she might have been delighted to date.

"You look great, Julie," he approved. "Got yourself acclimatized?"

"I think so," she replied ruefully. "Was I awful yesterday? To tell the truth I don't remember it very clearly."

"You were out on your feet," Hal said. "But you were still the prettiest woman I'd seen in ages. Tonight, all bright-eyed again . . . well! Words fail me."

"Thank you." Her morale lifted a little, though she drew her shawl more closely around her, disturbed by the way his eyes roamed so boldly. Compliments were fine, but too much flattery was to be suspected.

Hal had a taxi waiting to whisk them through the busy evening streets to the theater where a play called *Rain before Seven* was running. They had time for a drink in the foyer bar before taking their seats, and before too long Julie found herself hemmed in by other people in semidarkness, with Hal beside her leaning heavily on the connecting arm of their seats so that she could hardly move without touching him. He kept whispering in her ear and eventually laid his arm along the back of her seat, making her feel even more uncomfortable. All her instincts were on guard, and she knew that if she had had any sense, she would never have gone out with Hal Greaves.

Four

The play was a light comedy with only a small cast, amusing in its way but not so absorbing as to allow Julie to forget the close presence of her escort, so it was a relief when the lights went up for the intermission and she was able to escape that contact with Hal, if only to follow him to the crowded bar, where he had ordered more drinks.

"Enjoying it?" he asked.

"Yes, thank you," she replied, not entirely truthfully. "My folks will be green with envy when I tell them I've been to a West End theater."

"I'm only sorry it wasn't one of the top shows," Hal said, "but with so many tourists in town I was lucky to get tickets for anything. What do you think of Liz Bentham?"

In the dim lights, with chattering people crowding on all sides, Julie forced herself to meet his eyes. "Sorry?"

"Elizabeth Bentham—she's playing Sally." He took his program from his pocket, turning it to the page that showed pictures of the cast, including the dark-haired young actress who was playing the female lead. "That's her. Elizabeth Bentham."

"She's very good," Julie said. "Why, should I know her? Is she famous?"

Hal laughed. "No, not really. But I thought Nick might have mentioned her."

Her stomach contracted in a most peculiar way, but she hoped her face gave nothing away. "Nick? I don't follow."

"She's his girlfriend," Hal said.

Elizabeth Bentham's picture smiled up from the program, short dark hair curling around a classically beautiful face. She looked self-assured, sophisticated. Julie recalled a confident voice over the phone from Nick's apartment, and now there was a face to go with it, not to mention a curvaceous figure that the play's costumes did little to conceal. With a woman like that waiting at home, there was no wonder Nick had not been thrilled to spend time waiting at the airport for someone who, to him, was nothing but a nuisance.

"They've been together two or three years now," Hal was saying. "There was talk of them getting married, but Liz wants to concentrate on her career at the moment."

Very slowly she closed the program, smoothing the shiny cover with her hand. "Is she the reason you brought me to this particular play?"

"No! I told you—it was the only one I could get tickets for at short notice. But I thought, since you're going to be seeing a lot of Nick, you ought to be aware of the situation."

By the time she looked up, she had her expression under control. "What made you think I didn't know about it? I already knew he had a girlfriend. Not that it's any concern of mine. His private life is his own affair."

"Is it? Yesterday I got the idea you rather liked him. I sensed undercurrents. You know how it is. An observer notices these things, even if the people involved aren't consciously aware of them."

"I'd only known him a few hours!" she protested.

Hal eyed her levelly. "So I was mistaken?"

"You certainly were! Nick and I just happen to be

50

working colleagues. If you sensed undercurrents, why . . . why it must have been animosity. He hates being assigned to me, and he doesn't care if it shows."

"Well, that's a relief," Hal said, grinning and glancing around as a bell rang to warn of the imminent rising of the curtain. "Let's go back to our seats, shall we?"

Julie did not enjoy the rest of the play, mainly because she was too busy watching Liz Bentham to follow the twists of the plot and also because Hal kept making low-voiced comments, leaning much too close for her liking. She spent most of the time wishing the play would end, for the theater seemed claustrophobic and airless.

When at length they emerged into the cool, neon-lit streets of London's West End, Julie breathed deeply and gratefully of the fresh air, wanting only to get back to her hotel.

"Where shall we eat?" Hal asked. "The restaurants will be crowded. It would be much easier to relax back at my place. I do a mean steak and salad, and I've left some wine chilling."

Knowing full well what a trip back to his place might lead to, Julie glanced around at the signs along the road and saw a Chinese restaurant not far away. "It would be more fair if I treated you to dinner, since you bought the theater tickets. I love Chinese food. How about that place over there?"

"If you like." His smile was knowing and slightly rueful as he took her arm and led her across the road, dodging among the slowly moving cars.

By the time they had finished their meal, all her doubts about Hal Greaves had been confirmed. Though full of charm and smiles, he had little about him that really appealed to her, and she suspected he had taken her for a lonely foreigner who would be an easy conquest. When he suggested that they might go back to his place for a nightcap, Julie refused, making it quite clear that he had missed his guess about her.

Surrounded by groups of foreign tourists jabbering away in Swedish, German, even Japanese, Julie and

Hal walked back toward Piccadilly Circus, passing a place where an artist offered quick sketches of passersby. A nearby booth sold badges, trinkets, and cardboard bowler hats. Many of the souvenir shops remained open, spilling warm air into the street, where the night was alive with movement. Lights flickered and changed across the faces of the crowd and the shining flanks of cars.

"How about a souvenir of our first date?" Hal asked, taking her arm to guide her into an open-fronted arcade crammed with racks of T-shirts and jeans, crazy hats and all manner of novelty items, many of them commemorating the royal wedding, and many of those quite hideously tasteless. The blare of pop music was deafeningly loud, making it impossible for Julie to hear what Hal was saying as he held up various items, including a T-shirt bearing a picture of Prince Charles and his fiancée.

"Very scarce!" he shouted in her ear. "We've only got a few left."

"How much?" Julie yelled back.

"A present!" He signaled to the young assistant, who nodded. The T-shirt was thrust into Julie's hands and, dazed by the battering at her eardrums, she allowed herself to be propelled back into the rainbow night.

"That's my shop," Hal explained. "You'll look good in that shirt—and that's why you're here, isn't it? Because of the wedding? We're doing a bomb with Charles and Di stuff. It's a real bonanza."

That remark alone was enough to make Julie dislike him. His only interest in the wedding was a mercenary one, and from what she had seen of the goods in his shop, he was making his fortune from cheap trash. It was all to do with profit, not affection or respect for the prince and his bride-to-be.

As he walked her back to the Delphinia, she rehearsed a suitably caustic speech in case he should ask to see her again, but he left her at the hotel steps with nothing but a promise to call her. Obviously he had got the message.

It had been an uninspiring evening—the wrong

man to begin with, not to mention the depressing sight of Nick's gorgeous girlfriend. Julie told herself she had no hope of competing with Liz Bentham, even if she had been the type to attempt to break up Nick's relationship with the actress. The only thing to do was to stop thinking about Nick Tregarron as anything other than a colleague.

But at least she now had a Charles and Di T-shirt. She unfolded it and shaped it against herself in front of the mirror. Grinning, she remembered the beloved Beatles T-shirt of her teens. She had worn it with such pride! Just as she intended to wear this with pride—to show how much she loved the royal romance.

She had just climbed into bed and was about to turn out the light when the phone rang sharply beside her. Wondering if it might be her mother calling from the States to check up on her, Julie glanced at her watch and tried to work out what the time would be in Philadelphia, but the calculations stopped, and a warm flush suffused her whole body as Nick Tregarron's baritone voice said in her ear, "Hello? Julie?"

Striving to remain casual when all her nerves were quivering, she replied, "Hi, Nick."

"Oh, you *are* there," came the relieved reply. "I was about to send out search parties. This is the fourth time I've tried to get hold of you this evening."

"Is it?"

"Well, you did ask for me to call you, didn't you? I was beginning to think something terrible had happened."

"Then set your mind at rest," Julie said. "Actually, your lady got the message wrong. I didn't ask for you to call me, I said I would try again later."

"Oh, I see. Was it something important?"

"No, not 'specially. I just thought I should get in touch. I . . . was expecting to see you today." Even as the words came out, she could have bitten her tongue sooner than have him hear the wistfulness she had inadvertently revealed.

"Missed me, did you?"

His lazy, mocking tone was so unexpected that she hesitated in confusion. "That wasn't what I meant! I've been too busy to give you much thought, if you want the truth. I had to make up for yesterday."

"Why, what happened yesterday?"

"I came back here and slept—all afternoon and evening. I was bushed. I guess it must have been jet lag." Through her edginess she remembered that she owed him an apology, though, now that the opportunity had come, words seemed inadequate. "If I was snappish with you, I . . . I'm sorry."

A small silence came from the other end, as if he were searching for a reply. At length he said slowly, "Do I gather you turned down Hal's invitation to go sightseeing?"

"I had to. I was asleep on my feet."

"But you went out with him tonight," he said, a hint of acerbity in his voice.

Instantly Julie was on the defensive. "Who told you that?"

"Your hotel receptionist. When I rang earlier she said you'd gone out with a fair-haired man, and knowing Hal the way I do, I guessed it would be him. When it comes to women, he has a one-track mind. So I thought I'd better keep calling to make sure you were okay."

"And who appointed you my moral guardian?" she demanded.

"Since I introduced the two of you, I felt responsible. He might easily have lured you back to his flat, and you're such a little innocent you might not have been able to cope."

That was just too much. The good old double standard. How he had the nerve to say such things when he was living with his actress friend, Julie did not know. "I had no idea Englishmen were so protective," she said with sarcasm. "He took it upon himself to warn me about you, too. Anybody would think I just fell off the Christmas tree. I'm a grown woman, you know."

"That," said Nick, "is what worries me. What, er . . . what was it Hal said about me?"

"Nothing much. We went to see a play called *Rain*

Before Seven. The lead actress was very good. You might tell her I said so."

After another long pause, he said expressionlessly, "I'll do that. Okay, I consider myself well and truly reprimanded. Forgive me for being concerned about your welfare. Good night."

Smoldering with a passionate mixture of anger and regret, Julie found herself listening to a dead line. Cursing under her breath, she slammed down the phone, snapped off the light, and curled into a ball of misery, not quite knowing with whom she was most angry—Nick, or herself.

She recalled complaining to her grandfather that all the men she met were dreary, but that was one adjective that could not be applied to Nick Tregarron. Maddening, yes. Cynical, overbearing, enigmatic . . . but not dreary. Whatever her logical mind might say, she had to admit that in his presence, or even simply listening to his voice over the phone, all her senses came totally alive.

And then it occurred to her that she still hadn't remembered to make arrangements for meeting him again. Darn it! Why did Nick Tregarron have the power to make her so confused?

The following morning she phoned the International Press office for the address of the jewelers who were making the wedding ring for Lady Diana.

"I'll put you through to information," came the voice of Maddie Venables. "How are you doing, Julie? Did you find Nick Tregarron?"

"In a way," Julie said, containing a sigh. "I talked to him on the phone, but he didn't say when he'd be turning up again. Having him 'help' me seems to have been a lousy idea."

"Gosh, how can you say that? I only wish I were in your shoes." Maddie sounded dreamy again. "By the way, if you're not busy tonight, how about coming over to the flat for a meal and a chin-wag?"

"A what?" Julie laughed.

"A chin-wag—a natter—a chat. You know, girl-to-girl stuff. My flatmate's going out, so there'll only be me, and I do hate spending Saturday nights on my own. Oh—I don't mean that's the reason I'm inviting you. I just thought you might like some company."

"I'd love it," Julie said sincerely.

"Oh, great! I'll give you my address, shall I? Have you got a notepad handy?"

"Ever know a reporter who didn't?" Julie said with amusement, pencil poised. "Go ahead."

Having written down Maddie's address and directions for taking the Tube, London's subway, to get there, she spoke to IP information and took note of the whereabouts of Collingwoods of Mayfair, the jewelers. When she consulted her map, she found that Conduit Street was within easy walking distance of her hotel, so she set out to find it, attired in comfortable jeans and proudly wearing her new T-shirt.

Collingwoods proved to be a discreetly opulent establishment off Bond Street, with white-tiled steps leading up to each of its two doorways, which both displayed the royal crest in full colors. In the arched window, three display cases each held a single necklace, but the entry was guarded by a large, uniformed man. Politely but adamantly he refused Julie permission to go inside to interview anyone. Yes, he said, it was true that the royal wedding ring was being made of Welsh gold, from a nugget that had furnished the raw material for other royal wedding rings, including those worn by the Queen Mother, Queen Elizabeth, and Princess Anne. But the doors of Collingwoods were firmly barred to anyone seeking secrets as to design and any other details. The guard was smiling, polite, and about as talkative as the sphinx.

Julie recalled that Hank Freeman had warned her she might encounter just such a wall of silence, but the phenomenon baffled her.

Moving on, she paused outside the window of another jeweler's, where a glittering display of engagement rings caught her eye. She wondered how it must feel to come to such a place with one's future husband to choose a token of a pledge of mutual love. Had Lady Diana come to Collingwoods with the prince, to sit in a quiet room discussing the relative merits of rubies and emeralds, gold or platinum, before deciding on the sapphire and diamond ring that now adorned her finger? Dreaming again, Julie found herself trying to visualize what her own special man might look like. Tall, of course, and preferably dark, with velvet-brown eyes and a habit of lifting one eyebrow . . .

She nearly jumped out of her skin when she glimpsed the reflection of just such a man walking slowly up to stand beside her.

"Well, hello," Nick Tregarron said evenly. "Fancy meeting you here."

Julie whirled to face him, an odd sensation quivering up her spine as she wondered if her thoughts had made him materialize. "What are you doing here?"

"Waiting for you, actually," he replied, though the look in his eyes asked questions about the sudden color that had flooded her face.

"How did you know I was here?" she demanded.

"I was on my way to your hotel when I saw you leaving, so I came after you. You're finding your way around very well. I'm impressed."

Beginning to recover her equilibrium, Julie said loftily, "It's all part of my job."

"Well, if you're working, why look so guilty? You weren't planning a smash and grab raid, I hope?"

"You startled me, that's all."

"I suppose I shall have to take your word for—" The sentence broke off as his glance flicked to her breast, though to judge by the scowl that darkened his face, it was not her curves that he found so arresting. "Where the hell did you get that thing?" he demanded, gesturing at her T-shirt.

"Hal gave it to me," she said defensively, her chin tilting in defiance. "You may be antiwedding but I'm not. I'm proud to be involved, even in a tiny way, and I don't care who knows it."

The velvet-brown eyes, which had just smiled with tenderness in her dreams, looked hard as pebbles now.

"I don't suppose it had occurred to you that there aren't many of those hideous things around?"

"Yes, I had noticed. Hal said they were scarce."

"Good grief!" Nick groaned. "Of course they're scarce! Buckingham Palace has forbidden any British manufacturer to make such offensive items, so the few there are have been brought in from abroad, but nobody with any taste is buying them. They're not very good likenesses, are they? And how would you like your face plastered across somebody else's chest? It's all right for pop stars, but this is the Prince of Wales and his lady."

Her face burned even more hotly as she said in a small voice, "I hadn't looked at it that way. I didn't mean any disrespect."

"No, I don't suppose you did," he conceded, sighing. "I'm sorry. It's not your fault, it's Hal's. You weren't to know. But before you go anywhere with me, I'd be grateful if you'd change your shirt."

"Go . . . with you?" she said faintly. "Where?"

"Wherever you'd like to go. You may have forgotten, but I *am* supposed to be your photographer. Why do you think I came looking for you?"

"I hadn't thought about it." He was doing it again, she thought in despair, getting her all mixed up. Being with Nick was a prospect that both dismayed and delighted her, but she was also annoyed that he had caught her wearing the T-shirt. Oh, damn! Why couldn't she be cool and poised with him—like Liz Bentham?

Fearing that he might read her inner turmoil, she took refuge in looking up and down the busy street, where not far off a boutique advertised summer bargains. "Excuse me."

"Where are you off to?" Nick called after her.

"I'm going to change this shirt!"

Searching frantically along a rack of mix-and-match tops, she chose the first one in her size, a green-striped shirt, and put it on in a dressing room. She came out wearing it and bought it at once, bundling the offending T-shirt into a shopping bag. She would never forgive Hal Greaves for making her look such a fool, she thought as she hurried out to find Nick leaning casually against a lamppost.

"Better?" she asked breathlessly.

"It's an improvement," he replied. "Though now you look like a stick of peppermint."

Julie's temper sparked, but she clamped the lid on it. There had to be some way of dealing with this infuriating man other than constantly rising to his bait.

"Gee, thanks," she breathed sarcastically. "Such old-world charm."

His eyes rested on her flushed face. Suddenly, they twinkled, and unexpectedly he laughed, a warm, deep sound that did peculiar things to Julie's nerve ends, especially when his glance softened and rested on her mouth.

"I'm glad you brought your smile along today," he said, then seemed to recollect himself and straightened, easing the heavy equipment case that was slung, as usual, over one shoulder. "So—where is it to be? Would you like to see Clarence House?"

"Oh, yes. That—that's where the Queen Mother lives, isn't it?"

"Right—and Lady Diana will be leaving for the wedding from there, if all goes to plan. Interested?"

"Lead on, MacDuff."

"Shakespeare, too," he commented dryly. "Except that it's 'Lay on, MacDuff.' But for a Philadelphian it's not bad."

"You're too kind," Julie said sweetly and was rewarded by another grin.

She walked beside him, pleased that they had found a sort of understanding. At least he wasn't so grim today, and a joking relationship was better than constant bickering. If only her heart wouldn't keep fluttering so, she might begin to enjoy herself.

With Nick as her guide the way seemed short. They used side streets, past the ancient small hatter's shop that boasted three royal crests, to the grey fortresslike bulk of Saint James' Palace, where red-coated guards stood at ease, their young faces still and impassive beneath their bulky hats of black bearskin. Then they turned a corner and entered one of the curiously quiet places that London afforded, a narrow street with wrought-iron gates open at the far end. To the left a big square house was guarded by more of the imperturbable soldiers in their scarlet and black. Here a small group of sightseers gazed curiously at net-curtained windows and at the high wall, beyond which a flower-trimmed balcony was visible.

"That's where the queen mum comes out to greet the crowds who always gather on her birthday," Nick said.

"Are these people waiting to see her now?" she asked.

"No, they've just come to stare—like you. You should see yourself, all bright eyed and awestruck. Tourist!"

Julie made a face at him, and he laughed at her, but this time she didn't mind. She was trying to imagine what this quiet road would be like on the wedding day, when Lady Diana would leave Clarence House in the glass coach, with her father beside her. Would she hold his hand for comfort in her nervousness?

With a screech of brakes, a police car drew up by the guarded gate, which swung open to allow a black limousine to emerge. A murmur of excitement ran through the crowd as the two cars swept by. Julie glimpsed a familiar face, a smile, a wave. She was waving back, along with the rest, before she fully registered the fact that she was looking at the Queen Mother. And then the cars were gone.

"It was her!" she gasped.

"Of course it was," Nick said. "Why do you think I brought you here at this precise moment? She'll be on her way for elevenses with the queen." He smiled at her bewilderment. "At eleven, all England takes its coffee break—though some still insist on tea."

"Really?" Round-eyed with amazement, she actually believed it in the moment before she registered his expression. "Oh, you're teasing me! You couldn't have known we'd see her. Who was the lady with her, do you suppose?"

"It looked like Lady Fermoy—she's been lady-in-waiting to the queen mum for years, and her close friend. She's also Lady Diana's grandmother. Which, when you think about it, is highly significant."

But Julie was too entranced to react to the implied sarcasm of the comment. "Oh, Nick!" she breathed. "I can hardly believe all this is happening!"

He shook his head at her indulgently. "You remind me of Alice in Wonderland."

"I really don't care. Laugh all you want. I'm just thrilled to be here. I can't wait for the wedding."

"Neither can I," he said. "When that's all over maybe we can get back to normal."

"You're just a miserable party-pooper," she retorted. "I refuse to let you get me down. Where now?"

"Well, Buck House is just down the road, and it's about time for the changing of the guard, if you'd care to join the gaping crowds."

"Buck House?" she asked. "What's that?"

"Oh, dear me," Nick said, giving a mock sigh. "I can see I'm going to have to educate you, my dear Philadelphian. I meant Buckingham Palace. But if you're not interested—"

"Just lead me to it!"

"I was afraid you might say that. All right. Follow me."

All in all, it was the best day Julie had yet spent in London. Her notebook was covered in scribbles, and Nick took several rolls of film as they watched the changing of the palace guard, all scarlet and gold, with mounted escorts and with a military band playing, to the delight of the crowds who gathered to watch the spectacle. After lunch, she and Nick called at the homes of some of the youngsters who were to be Lady Diana's attendants. They succeeded in getting interviews and pictures of India Hicks and little Clemmie Hambro, who at a wide-eyed five would be the youngest bridesmaid.

Finally, weary but satisfied that she had done a good day's work, Julie flopped into the one vacant seat of a subway car, while Nick strap-hung beside her.

"Are you aware that it's six o'clock?" he asked. "If I'd known you were such a slave driver, I'd have thought twice about giving up my Saturday."

Appalled, Julie glanced at her watch. She had promised to be at Maddie's apartment by seven-thirty, which left little time to bathe and change before catching the subway to the suburbs.

"I'll have to rush," she said.

"Oh, yes? Got an appointment?"

"I'm going out to dinner. Nick, I'm sorry to have kept you so long, but thank you. Have I ruined your weekend?"

His face was unreadable, his eyes veiled, as he shrugged. "No, I've done a fair amount of my own work, too. Anyway, that's what I'm here for, isn't it—to be useful? But if you've nothing urgent in mind, I will take the day off tomorrow. I like to spend my Sundays at home."

On Sundays, she thought, the theaters were shut, which meant that Liz Bentham would be at home, too.

"Of course," she said lightly, ignoring the sudden emptiness inside her. "I've got plenty of writing to do."

"Good."

Something had happened, Julie was sure. Something had cooled the air between them, though she couldn't decide what it was. The thought of Liz, perhaps? During the rest of the journey she tried to make conversation but received only terse replies. Nick watched the dark wall of the tunnel rush by, not glancing at Julie, not even sitting down beside her when the seat became vacant.

"I may as well get off here," he said as the train slid into a station. "I can make a connection for getting home. See you Monday, probably."

"Sure," was all Julie had time to say before he was gone.

She watched him stride away with other travelers,

making for the arched exit tunnel, and all at once she felt so miserable she could have wept. She stared out of the window as the train moved again, her reflection staring wanly back at her against the black background of the tunnel wall.

For no reason at all she recalled her grandfather saying, "You'll go far. You're an Elliott," as if being an Elliott made everything just perfect. But she must remember that her family expected great things of her. She must remember, too, that her stay in England was to be brief; she would be leaving the day after the wedding. So it was pointless to give way to a hopeless juvenile crush on Nick Tregarron. Apart from anything else, and even if he had not been heavily involved elsewhere, her family would not approve of him. They had in mind for her someone of standing—a doctor, a lawyer, an architect—certainly not a foot-loose photographer.

Oh, dear Lord! She sighed to herself. Stop dreaming, you fool! You're lonely, that's all. Nick has been kind, in his fashion, and he's become your guide in a foreign city, but that's no good reason to imagine anything else. Besides, he wouldn't look twice at you, not in that way. Not with the glamorous Elizabeth Bentham waiting at home for him.

Later that evening she took another subway out to Hampstead. Maddie's address proved to be the basement of what must once have been an elegant townhouse that was now converted into half a dozen apartments. Steps led down to a paved area, where a tub of petunias made a splash of color among the brick and concrete, and inside the apartment bright hangings and cushions lent an exotic air.

The plump redhead made a cheerful hostess, and soon Julie felt very much at home as they talked about their families, their ideas—and about Nick Tregarron, though Julie took care to maintain an appearance of disinterest when his name came into the conversation. Maddie might happily confess to a distant passion for him, but then Maddie wasn't entirely serious.

And Julie was. Arguing with herself had made no difference. Nick Tregarron aroused feelings that she had never experienced before, feelings that were half exciting, half frightening, and wholly perplexing—not the kind of thing she could joke with Maddie about.

The two talked so late that Julie missed the last train, and with the effects of the red "plonk" that Maddie poured so liberally, she was only too happy to sleep on the sofa for the night, though she woke with a headache, a crick in her back, and the depressing memory that Nick would be spending his day with Liz Bentham.

Julie passed her Sunday afternoon at International Press, typing up material for two articles and congratulating herself on having succeeded this far. At least she was producing copy, even if it was less than sensational.

She had just returned to her hotel when Nick phoned, still terse and offhand as he asked her about her plans for the next day and offered to drive her down to Chatham, where the wedding cake was being made.

"I'm not sure it will get you an interview, but we can try," he added.

"That sounds great," she replied. "I've been thinking I ought to do some sleuthing in that area."

"Good, then we'll do it tomorrow. I shan't be available on Tuesday, I'm afraid. My plans will take me out of London."

The news made her feel dejected—and not only because of her work. "Where are you going?"

"Sandringham," he said.

"But . . . isn't that the queen's private estate? Lady Diana grew up in a house there."

"Park House, yes. Of course, if you'd care to come with me—"

"Would I!" she exclaimed. "Though if you'd prefer not to have me tag along, just say so."

"It won't make any difference to me," he told her. "But it's a longish drive, and I want to start early. We'll talk about it tomorrow. Have you, er, had a good day today?"

"Fine!" she said brightly. "I've been at the office."

"And did you, um, enjoy your dinner date?"

"Yes, thank you. I had a fine time. How's your day been? Relaxing, I hope?"

"Like most Sundays," he replied enigmatically. "So I'll pick you up about nine tomorrow—to go to Chatham."

"Yes, fine."

After he had said goodbye, she sat gloomily chastising herself for her constant use of the word fine when everything was far from fine. Nick had sounded distant, and not only because of a bad connection. Probably he hadn't been alone. But what on earth had gone wrong yesterday? What had she said, or done, to drive the wedge back between them, just when they were getting along so wonderfully? It really doesn't matter, she told herself crossly. He's not for you. You're just mooning. Pull yourself together, Julie Elliott, and get on with your job.

The lecture seemed to have a good effect—for at least five minutes.

Five

She was, she decided, going to have to play it cool and detached if she was to retain any pride whatsoever; Nick must never guess what a fool she was making of herself over him. But when he appeared the next morning, the very sight of him caused upheaval inside her, a swooping, giddy sensation that left her feeling on edge.

While they drove the forty miles to Chatham, mostly through the London suburbs before they reached the green countryside of the North Downs of Kent, their conversation was spasmodic, touching only on the business at hand. Nick warned her that they couldn't even be sure of getting inside the naval base, whose cookery school had been invited to make the wedding cake because of Prince Charles's close connections with the Royal Navy.

HMS Pembroke proved to be a shore station set near the estuary of the river Medway. When they arrived at the gate, Nick told Julie to wait while he climbed out. He exchanged a few words with the guard, who eventually allowed them through.

"What did you say to him?" Julie asked.

"I just gave him our names. Actually I phoned earlier, and they said they would see what they could do. They're used to press interest by now."

That all sounded logical, and Julie thought no more of it. Chief Petty Officer David Avery, who was responsible for making the cake, met with them.

As yet, its design and precise ingredients were a secret, he said, but he could reveal that it would contain all the usual ingredients of a rich fruitcake—eggs, butter, nuts, fruit . . .

"I read somewhere that you used one hundred fifty eggs," Julie said.

CPO Avery smiled. "Did you? Well, it may be somewhere near right."

But he wouldn't tell how many tiers the cake would have or whether it would be iced all in white. Instructions had told him to make a "pretty" cake, he said, and Lady Diana had approved the design, though she had said that she had never tasted naval rum, which His Royal Highness had requested should be included among the spirits added to the mix. The cake was being made in Kitchen Fourteen, under strict security conditions, and it had taken four men two whole days to check all the fruit that had gone into it.

"It must weigh a ton," Julie commented.

"No, a bit under two hundred pounds," the chef corrected. "That's including the marzipan and icing, of course."

"Are you pleased with the result?" she asked.

"I hope I shall be, when the last touches are added. Then our only worry will be getting it safely to London without breaking it."

He would not say when this journey was to take place or what sort of vehicle would carry the cake. All her questions were answered with smiles and evasions.

As she and Nick drove back to London, Julie said, "I'm beginning to feel like a spy after State secrets. Nobody minds me asking, but nobody will say anything definite."

"He probably hasn't even told his wife," Nick said.

"But at least you got your interview, and your pictures. That's all you can hope for, until the details are released, and when that happens everyone will know. You'll only have to read the morning papers."

"I keep doing that, but they don't seem to know any more than I do." A sigh escaped her as she leaned back in her seat. "Hank Freeman warned me about it, but I didn't believe him. I mean . . . who cares if the whole world knows the cake recipe?"

"What gets me is why the whole world wants to know it in the first place," Nick said sourly. "Doesn't it occur to you that we've wasted practically an entire day, not on something of earth-shattering importance but on chasing after the recipe for a giant fruitcake? When half the world is starving?"

"Well, if they gave it away it wouldn't feed that many," she argued. "There's too much gloom and doom around. We all need a touch of glamour and romance."

"I don't," he retorted.

She glanced covertly at him, seeing his strong hands on the wheel, his tanned profile, the dark hair that curled around his ear, and she was caught unaware by a wave of tenderness. Why was he so averse to the very idea of the royal wedding? Was it because he wished for a wedding of his own but his girlfriend was too busy building her career, as Hal had said? Liz Bentham must be out of her mind! In her shoes, Julie wouldn't have refused to marry Nick Tregarron because of her career. These days a woman could combine the two.

"That's no good reason for you to want to spoil it for everyone else," she said. "Oh, I've seen the correspondence in the papers—there are a few moaners who hate the expense, but it's mostly out of sour grapes and jealousy. If they had their way the world would be a uniform gray. You've only to walk around London to sense how the majority of people are really looking forward to the great day. It will be wonderful—all the pageantry and color, carriage processions and marching bands, and the bells ringing. . . . You should hear

Maddie Venables carry on about the subject. She's even worse than I am."

He shot her a dark, irritated look. "That takes some believing. And who's Maddie Venables? One of your friends stateside?"

"She's the receptionist at International Press," Julie said, surprised. "The little redhead you were so busy talking to that first morning."

"As I recall, we were just exchanging the time of day," Nick said. "I didn't bother to ask her name."

"That's typical!" she exclaimed. "Poor Maddie thinks you're the greatest thing since sliced bread, and you hardly even noticed her!"

"It's nice to know somebody thinks I'm wonderful," he returned. The trace of bitterness in his voice made her turn in her seat to look fully at him.

"Are you going to tell me what's wrong, Nick? I know there's something. I thought we'd started to be friends, but. . . . Is it something I said?"

He glanced at her again, with something like disgust in his eyes, but when he spoke she realized it was directed at himself. "No, of course it isn't. I don't mean to sound like a bear with a sore head. I'm sorry."

"Want to tell me about it?" she asked, sympathetically.

"About what?"

"About whatever it is that's making you uptight. I know you're not happy about having me trail around with you, but it's not just that, is it? Have you—have you had words with"—her lips wouldn't frame Liz Bentham's name, so she ended lamely—"with someone?"

"Only myself," he said tightly. "Forget it. It's not important."

Obviously he didn't feel like sharing it, not with her. Stifling a sigh, Julie returned her attention to the passing suburbs, then asked him to drop her off at International Press.

"I may as well get my piece about the cake written up, then I can get an early night—if we're still going to Sandringham tomorrow."

"Why not?" he said, shrugging. "You might as well see some more of the country while you're here."

"And I'd better not tell Maddie Venables about it," she added, still trying to cheer him up. "If she knows we're going off for a whole day, she'll be wild with envy. She's got quite a thing about you. Saturday night your name kept cropping up every few minutes."

"Are you trying to play go-between?" Nick demanded.

"No, of course not!" Rattled, she subsided into silence.

After a while, Nick said, "How come you saw the IP receptionist on Saturday night? I thought you had a date."

"Not exactly a date. I went over to Maddie's apartment for dinner. I thought I'd told you. We were so busy talking I missed the last train and had to sleep on her couch, but it was fun. She's a lovely person. But she's lonely, I guess, and a kind word from an attractive man can work wonders—not that she takes you seriously. You don't need to worry."

"I had no idea I had so much charisma," he said, and it seemed to be the truth. He was a very attractive man, but he didn't appear to realize it. Julie found that very endearing—in fact, the more she saw of Nick the more she found to admire in him, and the more it bothered her.

Quite what was showing in her face as these thoughts ran through her mind she wasn't sure, but she was disconcerted to find herself confronted by brown eyes that were alight with amusement in the moment before he returned his mind, and his gaze, to the road ahead. His mood had changed like lightning, and, not for the first time, she told herself she would never understand him.

Familiar landmarks began to appear, and soon the car was sliding to a halt outside the door of International Press.

"Thanks for the ride," Julie said, struggling with the door handle, which seemed to have developed a will of its own and wouldn't work. "I never expected to meet the man who actually made the cake. You must bring me luck. Oh—darn this thing, it's stuck!"

"Maybe it doesn't want you to go," Nick said in a low voice, making her be still, though she didn't dare look at him. She was aware of the intimate closeness in the car, his arm all but brushing hers. She had a feeling he was going to lean across and try the door for himself, which would mean touching. . . .

But a moment later Nick had climbed out and was striding around to open the door from the outside, giving her a little bow. Calling herself a fool for reading too much into his most casual remarks, she slid from the car into the quiet street.

"It does that sometimes," he said. "I must get it fixed. Julie . . ."

"Yes?" She glanced up, seeing him run a hand through his hair as he sought for words.

"Forgive me."

"For what?" she asked in bewilderment.

"For the way I've been behaving," he said, and unsettled every nerve in her body by placing both hands firmly on her shoulders. She knew she ought to say something, but at that moment her throat had ceased to function, every pulse pounding in response to his nearness. Even through her shirt his hands seemed to burn her flesh, making it tingle with nervous delight.

"And whatever made you think I didn't like your company," he added in an undertone, "it's not true. I'm not at all sorry that I let Jim Dawes talk me into doing this job."

Hoping he could not feel how she was trembling, Julie ran the tip of her tongue around suddenly dry lips, swallowed with difficulty, and replied, "That's nice."

"I think so," Nick said, a little smile tugging at one corner of his mouth. "So, I'll see you tomorrow at seven o'clock sharp. We'll stop for breakfast somewhere along the way."

His fingers tightened on her shoulders as he leaned to place the lightest of kisses on her brow, much as an

71

elderly uncle might have done. Except that Julie didn't feel like a niece—no, definitely not. She felt as though a switch had been thrown inside her, lighting her up, and she just managed to reply to his casual, "'Bye for now."

Then the car was moving away, nosing into the traffic along Fleet Street, leaving her shaken. Maybe she had dreamed all that, for he couldn't have meant it. He couldn't have!

But when she thought about it, she realized nothing very much had happened. Just a few softly spoken words, which she had probably misinterpreted, with an apology and a brief brush of lips against her forehead. Nothing! Then why did she feel as if the San Andreas fault had suddenly shifted inside her? She was being ridiculous!

Wrenching herself back to normality with an effort, she went into the office and applied herself to her work, but it was no good trying to ignore that something decidedly odd was happening to her, something she had never experienced before. She was falling in love with Nick Tregarron, but it wasn't the wonderful moonlight and roses experience she had dreamed about: it was frightening, because he wasn't free to feel the same way. And it was much, much too sudden.

Casting around in her mind for some shred of comfort, she told herself that she might have been mistaken about his relationship with Liz Bentham. Without doubt there was some sort of relationship going on—both Maddie and Hal had said so, and Liz had answered Nick's phone that day—but it was possible that it wasn't as deep as Julie had supposed, and that would make all the difference in the world.

She left the office at the same time as Maddie Venables, so the two walked to the subway together.

"Have you heard the queen mum isn't well?" Maddie said, worried. "She's canceled her engagements for three days as a precaution. Oh, I do hope she's better for the wedding. It wouldn't be the same without her there."

"It certainly wouldn't," Julie said, remembering the

sweetly smiling face that had looked out of a limousine at her only two days before. "What's wrong with her?"

"A temperature, they said. Nothing to worry about. But she's not a young woman any more and you can't help worrying. Everyone loves the queen mum. And what have you been doing with yourself today?"

Julie recounted her visit to Chatham, but in her mind the memory was overlaid by her personal troubles, and she could not resist asking, "Are you sure Mr. Dawes told you that Nick was as good as engaged?"

Maddie blinked behind her glasses, looking puzzled. "That's what he said. Why?"

"Oh, no reason. Just that he never talks about her, and I don't believe he's the kind of man who would pretend he was unattached if he wasn't." Though of course, she recalled, Nick was aware that she knew of his liaison with Liz Bentham. She had mentioned the actress that night on the phone, and he hadn't denied his acquaintance with her.

"All men can pretend when the mood takes them," Maddie said, giving a worldly-wise sigh. "It's the nature of the beast. But . . . he hasn't made a pass at you, has he?"

"Who, Nick?" Julie exclaimed. "Good heavens, no!" And that, she told herself sternly, is the truth, whatever your imagination might say. "I just wondered. But really I knew the answer. When I phoned him the other night, *she* answered."

The little redhead grimaced. "Ah well, living together is the 'in' thing these days. Not that I can see myself ever daring to do it. My mum would go spare if she found out. Besides, I always say if you're prepared to go to those lengths, you might as well go the whole hog and make it legal. But then we're a bit old-fashioned in my family."

"In mine, too," Julie said, sighing. "And if you ask me there are more of us about than the media would have people believe."

As they rode down on the subway escalators into smoke-smelling depths, she told Maddie she intended to spend the evening doing her homework before having an early night. She almost left it at that, but some demon of mischief made her add, "Nick's taking me to Sandringham tomorrow."

Behind the blue-rimmed glasses, Maddie's eyes narrowed thoughtfully. "Watch yourself," she advised.

"Oh, you needn't worry. He's the perfect gentleman."

Pausing where the tunnels divided, which would lead them to separate lines for their journey, Maddie said somberly, "It wasn't him I was thinking about. If you're starting to take an interest in his private life, you could be in trouble. He's quite a man, isn't he? And you're spending a lot of time with him. You're vulnerable."

For a moment Julie stared at her, wondering if she was a mindreader. "Yes, I know," she said quietly. "Don't worry, I'm aware of the pitfalls. But what can happen in the nine days I have left?"

"Too much," Maddie warned.

As they parted, Julie knew that her friend's advice was sound, but it was too late now to stop what was happening. Nine more days. . . . Time already seemed to be running out.

When she woke and looked out of her window the following morning, a light drizzle was falling over London. It matched her mood. Before her lay a long day alone in Nick's company, but if her heart leaped at the prospect, there were warning bells ringing in her head. Having taken a shower, she contemplated her wardrobe, wanting to wear something feminine solely for Nick's benefit, but in the end it was her head that won the battle, and she threw on a pair of jeans, a shirt, and a light, hooded parka, taking an extra sweater in case the day turned really cold.

Watching from the hotel lobby, she saw the MG draw up, Nick leaning to open the passenger door. A smile warmed his face, and she managed to greet him conventionally, despite the erratic jumping of her heart.

"That's what I like," he approved, "punctuality. With any luck we'll be away from the city before the rush-hour starts. Just fasten your seat belt. Comfy?"

"Fine. Let's go."

They seemed to have regained their easiness with each other, at least on the surface. For her part, Julie rode on a high, which was almost like being drunk, her senses attuned to Nick's every move and each nuance of his voice, though all he was doing was driving in his usual competent manner and chatting in a friendly way.

As they drove they talked about their respective careers, then Julie found herself telling Nick about her family and its history. She was talking far too much but she couldn't seem to keep quiet.

They stopped for breakfast in Cambridge, at a pleasant café where they sat opposite each other at a narrow table by a window with a view of the Gothic intricacies of some of the university buildings.

"One of your ancestors might have been educated here," Nick observed.

"Maybe so. Oh, I do wish I knew where the first J. J. came from! When I go home, I must do some research."

"Let me know how you get on. Perhaps I could help from this end, if you like."

Wondering if he meant that he wanted to keep in touch with her, Julie looked into brown eyes that held a disconcerting twinkle. "Would you?"

"Of course. I do quite a bit of traveling round and about."

"That's nice of you." She reminded herself that he was simply being friendly and she must be careful not to read any more into it. To him, she was just a passing stranger.

"You know—she leaned her elbows on the table, glad of the chance to gaze at him freely, seeing the unruly spring of his hair, the firm line of a tanned cheek, the dark lashes framing those velvet eyes—"I've told you a lot about myself, but you've hardly said a word about you. Are you a Londoner?"

75

Amusement twitched at his lips as he lifted an eyebrow in the habitual gesture that delighted her. "I am now."

"But you weren't born there?"

"No. My parents live in Berkshire. I have one sister, various aunts and uncles, assorted cousins . . . not very interesting."

"I was asking about you, not your family," she objected.

He gave her a lazy, devastating smile. "What is it you want to know, exactly? I thought you Americans were supposed to be forthright. Shall we start with basics? I'm thirty-two, the same age as Prince Charles, and I'm single."

The laughter in his eyes made Julie flush hotly. "That wasn't what—"

"Wasn't it?" Regarding her closely, he commented, "You've gone pink again. I thought modern girls had forgotten how to blush. Or has Lady Diana brought it back into fashion? I hope so. It's very fetching."

She was in danger of drowning in sparkling brown depths, she realized, straightening her back to put more distance between them as she stared at the spires of a building across the way. *I'm single*, he had said, but what did it signify?

Taking a deep breath, she made herself face him again and said it straight out: "Are you living with Elizabeth Bentham?"

The blunt question wiped every trace of humor from his face, leaving him startled by the forthrightness he had recently teased her with. "What gave you that idea?"

"She was at your apartment when I called the other evening. She must have been the one who told you I'd called."

Though she watched him closely, she could not guess the thoughts that went on behind his guarded expression.

"I've known Liz for a long time," he said carefully. "But to answer your question—no, we don't live together."

"I see." From the way he had framed that answer, she derived no consolation. Obviously Liz Bentham was very much a part of his life even if he wasn't anxious to talk about it.

"And you?" Nick asked. "Is there some bloke back in Philadelphia eating his heart out because you're away?"

"If there is, he's keeping it very secret. Look . . . I'm sorry. I shouldn't have asked. Shall we move on?"

The countryside beyond Cambridge seemed very flat, but at least the sun had come out by that time. Nick said they were approaching the fens, where great dikes had been dug to drain the marshes and leave rich, loamy soil that was ideal for arable farming. A few villages were clustered by the road, but on either side the land stretched out in great flat fields. But once into west Norfolk, the scenery became more undulating, and trees shimmered in full summer finery.

After stopping for coffee in the town of King's Lynn, which to Julie seemed awash with history, they drove the last few miles through gentle hills and woods, until Nick turned the MG down a side road where huge rhododendron bushes grew beneath the trees.

"This is all Sandringham estate," he said. "I want to take some shots of my own around here, and if you want to try to get a look at Park House, I suggest you take the car and scout around on your own. You do drive, I take it?"

"Yes, I do, but how do I find my way?"

"I've got a map in the glove compartment. We can meet up later and go into the grounds, if you like, though I'm afraid the house isn't open today. You'll get the atmosphere better if you take your time looking around."

They came in sight of huge wrought-iron gates set in a forbiddingly solid wall some seven feet tall, built of brick that was green with lichen, with trees lifting behind it. The wall seemed to go on for miles as Nick followed the road to an area where dozens of cars and buses were already parked among open woodland, with others lining up to find a place. Nearby stood a refreshment area and gift shop, built log-cabin style to blend with the trees and the high wall, where at a small gateway a line of visitors waited to pay their fee to enter the grounds of Sandringham House.

Pulling in to the side of the road, Nick leaned across to open the glove compartment, his shoulder brushing Julie's. She caught the clean scent of his hair. He took out a map and spread it across the driving wheel, pointing out their location on the road that circled the private area of the estate. Julie at once noticed the position of Park House, where Lady Diana had grown up practically within a stone's throw of the main Sandringham House. It was said that the royal family regarded this place as their real home because, along with Balmoral, it was the personal property of the queen. Edward VII, while Prince of Wales, had bought the property, raising his family here and bringing many VIPs to enjoy hunting, so Julie's research had informed her. Princes and princesses had been born here, and kings had died.

"Think you can handle the car?" Nick asked.

"I guess so," she said, lifting her eyes from the map to his face. "They won't be around today, will they? Prince Charles and Lady Diana, I mean?"

He gave her an indulgent smile. "I very much doubt it. How are you going to slant this—how she fell for the boy next door? Just don't ask me to take pictures of the place they're supposed to have met. A plain old field won't look very romantic. Anyway, she was just a kid. It was her older sister he noticed first."

"Until Diana grew up," she added.

"Is she grown up? Twenty's a bit young, if you ask me. Especially when the prince is my age."

"Nobody did ask you," she retorted, wondering if there was hidden meaning in his words. She was older than Lady Diana by over two years, but perhaps even that was too large a gap for Nick. Disturbed, she resorted to teasingly scolding. "The trouble with you, Nick Tregarron, is you have no romance in your soul."

"And you," he returned giving her a grin that made

78

her breathless, "probably still read fairy tales. But I'll be off. Come and get behind the wheel."

While she accustomed herself to the right-hand orientation of the car, he showed her how to adjust the seat for her shorter legs and leaned close to point out the basic switches and levers. His breath fanned her cheek so that she was hardly able to concentrate on what he was saying. Her fingers itched to touch him, but she kept them firmly curled in her palms, feeling relieved and yet disappointed when eventually he moved away to take his equipment case from the trunk.

Aware that he stood watching, Julie started the engine and selected first gear, looking up at him in satisfaction through the open window. He shook his head, smiling.

"Just remember to keep to the left," he instructed. "Be back here in—say half an hour?"

She managed to move off smoothly, sorry to be leaving him and yet glad to be able to breathe freely again. Not that she could forget Nick when she was driving his car, sitting in a seat still warmed by his body and assailed by the lingering scent of his after-shave.

To her disappointment she could not get near Park House, though she glimpsed it among trees beyond a locked gate. A large square house with tall chimneys, pointed gables and bay windows, it appeared to be empty now, but even so the sight of it set her imagination running. This had once been the family home of the Spencers, where Lady Diana with her sisters and brother had spent her youth, often in the company of Prince Andrew and Prince Edward, who had been more her age than Prince Charles or Princess Anne.

Driving on, Julie found that the wall continued, denying all view of what lay beyond it, and further on the impenetrable rhododendron bushes provided another excellent barrier. But after a while the growth became less dense, and only a fence protected the acres

79

of parkland beyond. Julie found herself approaching a hamlet of brown stone houses edged with brick, their small gardens ablaze with color, and to her surprise the fence paused at an open gateway opposite a row of cottages.

She stopped the car and got out, wondering if she dare walk right into the tree-dotted park. But as she hovered by the gate, a tweed-suited man wearing a porkpie hat appeared and strolled toward her, asking if she had business there.

"I was wondering if it would be possible for me to walk across to Park House," she replied. "You see, I'm a reporter, and—"

"Sorry," he broke in. "No one's allowed in here unless they have business with the estate manager. It's not permitted."

Although his expression was friendly, she had a feeling it might change if she persisted. He looked like a countryman, but he was probably part of the security operation.

"Do you work here?" she asked. "Have you met Lady Diana?"

"I've seen her once or twice," he admitted. "She's a sweet and lovely young lady, and I hope she and the prince will be very happy. Now if you wouldn't mind moving your car, miss, I'd be grateful. Why don't you go round to the main entrance if you want to see the gardens?"

"Can I get to Park House that way?" she asked hopefully, but he shook his head and informed her that the houses on the estate were private. All she might see were the queen's gardens and the little church.

Defeated, she returned to the MG and started slowly up the hill through the village. Soon she came to the tall brick wall again, where houses and stables lifted their roofs tantalizingly, and followed it to the public parking area.

As she climbed from the car beneath whispering trees, her depression lifted, for Nick was striding to meet her.

"Still in one piece?" he asked, smiling.

She gestured at the car. "Not a scratch on her."

"I meant you, not the car. Any luck?"

"Not much," she said, sighing. "You?"

"I've got most of the shots I wanted. Would you like to see the gardens while we're here?"

Having paid their entrance fee, they passed through the gate in the wall, into gardens rich with a colorful and varied display of flowers, plants, and shrubs, set among woodland glades, lawns and lakes, with the great house an ever-present reminder of the kings and queens who had lived here, each of them adding some personal touch to the gardens.

Julie visited the church, where people crowded at New Year's to see members of the royal family come for the service. Her only disappointment was that none of them were about on that day, though she kept feeling that at any moment she might walk into a prince or a duke.

"We'd better be thinking about lunch," Nick said as they walked away from the church back toward the gate in the wall. "I want to go somewhere else this afternoon. Or is there anything else you'd like to do here?"

"No, I don't think so—unless you could arrange for me to meet a real live lord, or someone."

For a moment he stood looking down at her, head on one side with the sun making the edges of his hair take on that reddish sheen. A little smile danced in his eyes. "I'm afraid you'll have to make do with me for now," he said at length, beginning to walk on. "Is that your highest ambition—to meet a real live lord?"

"Since Prince Charles is out of reach, I'd settle for that," she said lightly. "But if I had my druthers—"

"Your what?" he interrupted, raising an eyebrow.

"My druthers. You know—I'druther do this, or I'druther do that . . ." Remembering how he had poked fun at her ignorance, she peered up at him, feeling light-headed with joy in the day and his company. "I can see I shall have to educate you, my dear Englishman." She misquoted his own words back at him.

"Oh, touché!" He laughed and casually caught hold of her hand with warm fingers that sent a jolt like electricity up her arm to make her heart jump like a drunken frog. "You were saying—about your highest ambition? Your druthers?"

All she could think of was his hand clasped with hers, but with an effort she forced her mind back to the conversation. At that moment her only wish was for this day to go on, never ending, just the two of them away from everything. But since she could never say so, she sought refuge in the most unlikely thing she could imagine.

"I'd like to meet Prince Charles and Lady Diana and get invited to the wedding."

"Is that all?" He made owl eyes at her, laughing.

"If you're going to dream, dream big. That's my maxim."

But, oh, if only her real dreams would come true! They had nothing to do with royalty, with pomp and pageantry; they were all entwined around a dark-haired man with laughing brown eyes, a man who, even though he was holding her hand, was unattainable.

Leaving the royal estate, they found a pub in one of the nearby villages, an airy and comfortable place that offered simple inn food. Julie sat on a padded bench in a corner while Nick talked to someone at the bar as he ordered the meal and bought drinks, and though her eyes never left him, she was conscious of the unfamiliar burr of Norfolk accents around her.

When Nick returned, he brought a young man with him—a slim, athletic-looking man with dark hair and a wide smile.

"This is Michael Raines," Nick introduced his companion. "He's a carpenter, and apparently he did some work for the Spencers when they lived at Park House. Sit down, Michael. I'll bring you another beer."

Nick seemed to have a genius for being in the right place at the right time to encounter the right people, Julie thought as she chatted to the friendly Michael and listened to his anecdotes about his work and, in particular, his brief connection with the Spencer family and Lady Diana.

"One year on her birthday, when she was about nine or ten," he said, "her father arranged to have a camel brought from the zoo, and I built a ramp so that the children could climb up on the camel and have rides. And there was the time they wanted a treehouse. My mate and I went up to Park House to build it. It was a hot day, so we had our shirts off, and someone came and told us to put our shirts on again because the children were in the swimming pool and might see us—I suppose the sight of half-naked men might have upset them, or something." He laughed uproariously at the memory. "Still, there's not many can say they've built a treehouse for the future queen."

Julie made notes, in between eating her meal and drinking cold lager, and all the time she was thinking that some lucky star must have been shining when Jim Dawes persuaded Nick to help her. He seemed to possess some special magic to aid her in her assignment.

As they left the pub, she said something of this kind to Nick, who laughed. "I'm no magician. I happened to know that Sandringham workers often use this pub at lunchtime, so I asked the barman, and he called Michael over. It was just coincidence that he'd actually done some work for the Spencers." Pausing, he looked at her across the roof of the car, smiling in a teasing way. "I'll bet you still believe in Santa Claus. And elves, and magic dragons?" With that, he unlocked the MG and ducked inside.

Sighing to herself, Julie slid into the seat beside him. "Okay, so you think I'm an innocent—just an ingenuous, wide-eyed child. But I'm not, Nick."

"You are," he said softly, his voice touched by an odd nuance that she couldn't define. When she turned her head, she found him smiling at her as he reached to twist a lock of her hair around his finger, looking at the silky gold against his skin. "You pretend you're the tough career girl, got it all together and going places, but it's just an act, isn't it?"

"No!"

"No?" The feathery ends of the lock of hair brushed her mouth, and his eyes followed the movement, so that her lips tingled and softened. Afraid that he would see her response, she twisted her head away, slapping at his hand, thankful when he released her hair.

"And you expect me to believe you're not an innocent?" he said with gentle irony. "You panic every time I get near you."

Panic? Was that what it looked like? Thoroughly unnerved, she flung herself around to face him. "I do not!"

"Yes, you do. And don't cry, for heaven's sake!"

"I'm not crying!" she snapped, and instantly proved herself a liar. Stupid tears scalded behind her eyes, making her blink and turn away.

"Oh, hell!" he groaned, his hand touching her hair again, stroking as if to comfort her, rubbing her shoulder and her neck. "Julie . . ."

"I'm not a child," she muttered, turning drowned eyes to his.

"I know that. I was teasing you. I didn't mean—" He was watching her mouth again, lifting a hand to brush a gentle thumb across her lips while his other hand suggested she move closer. She found herself obeying, drawn as if by magnetism until nearness drove his face out of focus and she closed her eyes, lifting willing lips as he kissed her. Nothing else existed. Only Nick, the warmth of him, the strength of his arm about her, and his mouth tender but insistent, while her mind whirled to the dizzying beat of her pulse.

When he released her she stared at him breathlessly, her head and heart thudding with disbelief. He moved away, cleared his throat, and sat with hands on the wheel and eyes narrowed as he gazed out of the windshield.

"Point taken," he said eventually in a voice that was not quite steady. "You're certainly not a child. Will you get the road map out? I'd like you to navigate for me."

Six

As had happened earlier, when after breakfast
neither of them had mentioned Elizabeth Bentham
again, so now neither of them referred to that un-
guarded moment in the pub parking area. But as they
drove through the green countryside, Julie kept remembering it, and every time she did so hot blood
came tingling through all the tiny veins beneath her
skin, and her heart pounded until she felt almost ill.
She didn't even dare wonder what it had meant,
because reason told her it had meant nothing. It had
been a temporary aberration for both of them. He had
been trying to comfort her, that was all, and he
couldn't have known how it would affect her.

He seemed to be in a hurry, driving very fast on open
stretches of road. There were no highways in that area.
Country roads twisted and turned among fields where
corn was ripening and cows grazed in the shade of
stately trees, across more miles of flat fenland. Then
after they bypassed the town of Peterborough, the
countryside changed again, and there were hills and
woods and streams in pleasant valleys, with villages
nestling amid summer greenery and church spires
rising above dark stands of yew.

"It's beautiful," Julie said, sighing. "So peaceful. Oh, I wish I had more time to explore England."

"Maybe you'll come back some day," Nick replied.

"Yes, maybe."

Hoping to conceal the heaviness in her heart, she stared out of the side window at lovely meadows and coppices. She promised herself that she would come back some day, but she knew it woldn't be the same. Nothing would ever be the same again.

Lost in her thoughts, she forgot to navigate for him, but Nick apparently knew which roads he needed. Julie gave in to enjoying the scenery and reading the evocative names on the signposts. Oundle. Raunds. Great and Little Billing. Buttock's Booth. And then the busy streets of Northampton. As they came out into the countryside again, another sign caught her eye.

"Althorp Hall?" she queried, a catch in her throat. "Isn't that—"

"Earl Spencer's place, yes," Nick agreed. "And you pronounce it 'Altrup.'"

"Is that where we're going?"

He sent her a quick grin. "You've seen Lady Diana's childhood home, so I thought you might want to see her ancestral home, too."

"Oh, Nick . . . thank you."

His only reply was a smile, but it said enough.

Althorp Hall. There it was, sprawling elegantly behind a wide stretch of lawns and gravel driveways, its parking lot crammed with buses and cars as hundreds of tourists, their brochures open, milled around the gardens and wandered curiously in the house. Lady Diana's name was whispered frequently. This was where her family lived now, where the Spencers had lived since the time of Henry VIII, though their lineage went much further back into the mists of England's history.

Nick and Julie joined the murmuring throng to look at great rooms full of priceless furniture, paintings, and porcelain, and to climb the four-hundred-year-old staircase to a portrait gallery that stretched for one hundred and eleven feet, so the guidebook said. Julie found it difficult to imagine what it must be like to live in a stately home amid such grandeur.

As they returned to the main hall, Nick went across to speak to one of the guides and turned to call Julie over, asking her to follow him.

"Where are we going?" she asked.

"You'll see," he said mysteriously, leading the way to an unobtrusive door marked private.

It had been a day of surprises, but nothing had prepared Julie for finding herself in the private apartments of Althorp Hall, where Earl and Countess Spencer were waiting. She recognized them at once from their photographs and was astonished when they greeted Nick warmly, including her in their welcome, and sent for tea to be served.

She was so overcome with amazement that she forgot to take out her notebook until the earl gently told her she must feel free to write notes if she wished. He and his wife were charming, talking about Lady Diana with fondness and even showing Julie some photograph albums, with Diana Spencer gold-tooled on the covers, full of snapshots that the earl himself had taken as his daughter was growing up. Those snapshots would have brought a fortune on Fleet Street, Julie knew, but the earl guarded them with tender jealousy and seemed to regret the few he had allowed Buckingham Palace to release for publicity. He adored his youngest daughter and seemed a little sad that she could not have married some ordinary young man instead of becoming almost public property as the wife of the heir to the throne.

The meeting lasted nearly an hour before the earl bade his visitors goodbye. Julie stammered her thanks, clutching the precious notebook that was now full of exclusive quotes. Hank Freeman would never believe it, she thought dazedly.

As she and Nick emerged from the private door, she was aware of a flurry of interest among the tourists, which subsided at once when people realized they were not members of the Spencer family.

"How on earth did you manage that?" she breathed.

"A phone call," Nick said, as if arranging a meeting with the royal bride's father and stepmother were the simplest thing in the world. "I took some publicity stills of Althorp for them a while back, and they were very nice to me, so I thought I'd call and tell them I'd be bringing you down today. Having tea with them was their idea." As he surveyed her shining face, a slow smile tugged at his lips. "They're only people, Julie. Just like you and me."

She was so full of emotion that if she had had the courage she would have flung her arms round his neck and kissed him. He *was* a magician. He was probably the most beautiful, wonderful man in the world, and she was crazy about him. But all she could think of to say was a heartfelt, "Thank you, Nick. My editor will think I'm a genius, but if it hadn't been for you—"

"Oh, you'd have found some way," he said, shrugging as they reached the gravel path outside the house. "I didn't come here entirely for your benefit. I've got some great shots of the suckers who are paying a pound a head on the off-chance of catching a glimpse of the Spencers. Althorp's never been as popular as it is this year."

"You make it sound as though they arranged the wedding just to make money," she commented, a shadow clouding her delight. "Why are you so cynical?"

"I'm just trying to keep the thing in perspective," he replied. "Not everybody's like you, floating on cloud nine."

Tossing her hair, she swung around and marched back in the direction of the parking area. She had asked for that, she supposed. The day had passed in a fog of euphoria, not just from the excitement of seeing Sandringham and Althorp, and meeting the Spencers; no, it had all been intensified because of the way she felt about Nick.

Now he had reminded her of reality. They had to go back to London, where she must turn this glorious day into prose suitable for the *Philadelphia Star*, and

Step out of your world and enter

CIRCLE OF LOVE

the Circle of Love.

Treat Yourself to a New Romance

A new romance is just what you need. A Circle of Love romance. They're better-written romance novels, *full of intriguing men. Exciting international locales. Fantasies of never-ending love.*

Circle of Love romances are unlike any romance novels you've ever read. They're more compelling, more absorbing, and more satisfying page after page.

Receive the Next Six Titles Absolutely FREE

Now you can receive the next six Circle of Love romances absolutely free. It's your introduction to the Circle of Love Reader's Service. Just send in the card at right. Then we'll rush you the next six *all-new* Circle of Love titles. They're yours to keep whether or not you decide to continue the Reader's Service monthly program.

But if you enjoy the great reading, the convenience of home delivery, and *no* postage and handling charges, you can continue your membership simply by paying $10.50 for each shipment of six romances. You can even have each month's shipment of six titles charged automatically to your VISA or Mastercard account each month when it is shipped.

So don't miss next month's titles. *Send no money now.* But mail the postpaid card today.

Dear Reader:

With all the romance novels available, finding consistently satisfying reading is still not easy.

In Circle of Love romances, you're assured better writing. The stories are more suspenseful and more realistic. The characters are more genuine. And the romance is more satisfying from beginning to end.

Now you can enter the Circle of Love each month with the convenience of this no-risk offer.

Cordially,

Cathy Camhy

CATHY CAMHY *for Circle of Love*

Membership Application

☐ **YES.** Please send me FREE and without obligation the next six Circle of Love romances. Then send me the next six together with an invoice for $10.50. There are no charges for shipping and handling. The first six books are mine to keep whether or not I decide to continue my membership. There is no minimum number of books that I must buy, and I may cancel my membership at any time.

SIGNATURE _____

NAME _____

ADDRESS _____

CITY _____ STATE _____ ZIP _____

Payment Options: (check one)

☐ Charge each regular shipment to my: ☐ Bill Me
                                                11015
    13011 ☐ Mastercard   ☐ VISA

_____

   (Credit Card Number)   *expiration date*

Send no money now—but mail today

This offer is good only in the U.S.   A 123

tomorrow there were other stories to be found. And there was always Liz Bentham.

She longed to know exactly how Nick felt about his actress, but she had almost betrayed herself once by asking personal questions, and she shied away from a repetition of that indiscretion. Maybe he already guessed. Maybe that was why he had kissed her—because his ego sensed a conquest and couldn't resist taking a chance, even if he was "practially engaged" to another woman. She didn't want to believe it, but common sense told her that was her heart talking. A woman could always fool herself if she wanted something badly enough.

London blazed with light in the darkness when they arrived back, after stopping for dinner on the way. Around the city great billboards shouted wedding congratulations from one business or another, while flags and flowers spread wider with every day that passed. Julie was reminded of the night she had arrived in London, when Nick had driven her back from Heathrow Airport, except that her feelings had undergone a transformation. Then he had just been a puzzling stranger: now he was someone very important to her, though she could hardly claim she knew him or understood him. What she felt was a matter of chemistry, not of cool thinking. And since chemistry worked best with proximity, she decided it might be wise to find some excuse not to see him for a while.

By chance the space outside the Hotel Delphinia was clear that evening, and Nick drove her right to the steps, where he switched off the engine, leaving them in near-darkness.

"What have you got planned for tomorrow?" he asked.

"Jim Dawes is trying to arrange an interview with the Emanuels," she said. "They're the couturiers who are making the wedding dress."

Turning toward her, he shook his head, just visible against the blue glow from the hotel sign. "You're a trier, I'll give you that. They won't tell you anything new."

"I won't know that until I ask, will I?" she replied calmly enough, though inside she was so tense that she could feel herself trembling. "Anyway, there'll be no need for pictures. I've already checked that IP has some on file—and some photographs of the coaches, since I'm intending to visit the Royal Mews tomorrow afternoon. So you can do your own thing. I expect there's plenty you want to do, without following me around in quest of all the 'paraphernalia' you despise so much."

He made no reply. In the darkness she couldn't see his expression, but she was aware of being close to him in the confines of the MG, and as the silence lengthened, her nerves began to jump.

"Well, I'll say good night," she said, reaching for the door handle. "And thanks again. It's been a very productive day."

"I'm so glad."

Hearing the edge in his voice, Julie tried to open the door and nearly broke into a sweat when the handle stuck again. But after a moment it gave, and cool air rushed in. She leaped out thankfully, feeling as if she had escaped from some danger that left her pulses pounding.

But as she hurried for the steps, a man emerged from the hotel—a man whose slender form and fair hair she recognized with a sinking heart.

"Just the girl I'm looking for!" Hal Greaves exclaimed, smiling. "I've been asking for you at reception. I thought we might have a drink together."

Before she could form an answer, the car door slammed behind her, and Nick loomed up in the blue-lit shadows, saying coldly, "She's tired. We've been out since seven this morning."

Hal glanced at him in surprise, then smiled again at Julie. "Tomorrow, then. How about dinner?"

"Oh . . ." She hesitated, sensing the anger in Nick as though the air around him were vibrating. "Thanks, Hal, but I'm going to be awfully busy. With only a week to go before the wedding, I just don't know when I'll have any free time."

"You can't work sixteen hours a day," Hal argued. "Tell her, Nick. She needs some free time."

"I believe you heard what she said," Nick replied in a charged undertone.

Looking him up and down thoughtfully, Hal stuck his hands in his jacket pockets. "Yes, I heard, mate. I'm not deaf. Nor am I stupid. How's Liz these days?"

"Liz is very well, thank you," Nick said even more ominously, and from the corner of her eye Julie saw Nick's hands clench and unclench, while a muscle jumped in his jaw as if he were gritting his teeth.

A thin smile stretched Hal's lips. "I'm glad to hear it. All right, I'll let you get your beauty sleep, Julie. But I'll be in touch—sometime when this gorilla isn't around. 'Night."

He stepped lightly away, becoming a shadow among other shadows, his footsteps echoing around the tall buildings, and Julie released the breath she hadn't realized she was holding.

"I thought you two were friends!"

"We know each other," Nick said tersely. "That doesn't make us friends."

"And it doesn't give you the right to make decisions for me, either!" she cried, the tensions of the day bursting out in anger. "I'll see who I like! You know what you've done? You've made him think you're jealous."

A tiny hope in her heart begged him to confirm it, but his short laugh killed that hope. "Jealous? I was trying to protect you. Hal thinks he's God's gift to women. By turning him down you'll only make him more persistent, unless you convince him he's on the wrong track. That's the way he is. If you knew anything about men—"

"I know a darn sight more than you seem to think!" she said furiously.

"Do you?"

His hands shot out and fastened on her shoulders, whirling her around into the deep shadow by the hotel steps. Before she could do more than gasp a protest, he was kissing her, his arms tightly about her, preventing her from struggling while one hand tangled in her hair. She squirmed in his grasp, trying to wrench her head away, but his lips moved across her cheek and down her throat, warm and curiously tender despite the punishing strength of his arms. A shudder ran through her, turning her muscles to jelly as the desire to fight him off began to wane.

"Nick!" It was meant to be a protest, but it came out on a sigh as she gave in to the need to lean on him weakly, letting her body melt against his.

A thumb tilted her chin, and he searched her face in the dimness before slowly letting his mouth meet hers again, not angrily this time but sweetly, achingly. Her lips softened and parted as a wave of longing filled her, and her arms slid up to fasten behind his neck.

When he released her she was shaking, her hands resting on his chest, feeling the quickened beat of his heart.

"You think you know about men?" he said hoarsely. "You're naive, Julie. Like a trusting child. For all you know I could be as bad as Hal."

"You're not!" she gasped, snatching her hands away from him in horror.

"How can you be sure of that? How much do you really know about me?"

She shook her head frantically, not believing that this nightmare was happening. "Why are you doing this?" she whispered in anguish. "Why, Nick?"

"Because it's time somebody told you what a risk you're taking. It pays to be cautious in this world. Don't take everything at face value."

Unable to take any more, she brushed past him and made for the comparative safety of the steps, from where she looked down at him, hurt and humiliated.

"Thanks for the advice," she said bitterly. "I just hope I never get as cynical as you are. There has to be room for trust in the world—yes, and room for dreams and a sense of wonder. Okay, so you risk being hurt, but if that happens you pick yourself up and try again.

You don't stop believing. At least, *I* don't, and I hope I never will."

Without waiting for a reply she hurried away, hoping that her tears would not show in the softly lit foyer. Her lovely day had ended in ruins. Nick had taken all her illusions and ripped them to shreds. But at least he had achieved his object—he had made her come down out of the clouds.

With only a week left before the wedding, that Wednesday morning's newspapers ran noticeably more items in connection with the event. Julie's depression made her notice that one or two controversial notes were creeping in—Spain objected to the royal couple's choice of their claimed territory, Gibraltar, as a starting point for their honeymoon cruise, and Nancy Reagan's announced intention of not curtseying to the queen was making a few waves.

But there were happier notes, such as a piece about the sprig of myrtle that Lady Diana would include in her bouquet from a bush planted by Queen Victoria after her marriage to Prince Albert. The newspapers were also full of stories about a game of cricket in which the English team had won a historic victory, but Julie took scant notice of those because, to her, cricket was a mystery. She was interested only in wedding details, and she only hoped she was choosing the most interesting to pass on to her readers. To cover everything would be a hopeless task.

Calling Jim Dawes, she learned that the Emanuels, Lady Diana's couturiers, had agreed to try to fit her in to their busy schedule if she called at their Brook Street premises that morning.

"They said they were too busy at first," the bureau chief informed her, "but a few minutes ago a secretary rang and said they might be able to fit you in. I don't know what made them change their minds, but be there on time or you might lose your chance."

So luck was still with her, at least professionally.

Through pouring rain she made her way to Brook

Street and was surprised to find it crowded with waiting people, who all stood around a small corner salon decked with bunting. In the narrow side street, shoppers, office workers, newsmen, and even a cameraman with a hand-held TV camera had attention fixed on a dark blue door sporting a flowered garland. Just as Julie came within sight of the door, an umbrella was raised outside it, the door opened, and out came Lady Sarah, the oldest of the Spencer daughters, followed by a smiling Lady Diana. They were accompanied by two men whom Julie guessed to be detectives.

She could not take her eyes off the radiant bride-to-be, who looked even prettier than her photographs and immensely happy, even if she had lost weight with prewedding tensions. She wore a blue silk suit with pink lapels, cuffs, and a belt, and as the crowd called out in greeting, she stepped into a gray car and was whisked away, leaving Julie breathless with pleasure. But as the car sped away, she cursed her ill luck—that was probably the one time she would see Lady Diana clearly, and Nick was not there to take photographs.

Julie was not the only reporter anxious to interview David and Elizabeth Emanuel after what was probably the last fitting for the wedding dress. She found herself crammed into an upper sitting room, jostled by her fellow journalists while the two young designers stood backed into a corner facing the TV camera and a score of would-be interviewers.

"The dress isn't quite finished yet," Elizabeth Emanuel was saying. "I'm superstitious about finishing things too soon."

Yes, Lady Diana liked the dress, and if she was happy the Emanuels were happy.

After a short while the crush subsided, as those after "hot" news departed, leaving just a few feature writers, most of them foreign, like Julie. They asked questions that the young couple had obviously answered, or evaded, a hundred times before. Smiling but not entirely relaxed, the Emanuels sat on a chaise longue,

Elizabeth in pink with white polka dots, David wearing a red shirt.

Elizabeth revealed that her father had been a GI who had married an Englishwoman and stayed in England after the war.

"Our association with Lady Diana started with a photo session for Vogue magazine," David said. "As it turned out, Lord Snowdon was taking pictures of Lady Diana, and she liked the clothes we sent. After that she bought several of our outfits, including the off-the-shoulder black taffeta that caused so much comment. She looked stunning in that."

"Are you going to surprise us with the wedding dress?" someone asked.

They glanced at each other questioningly. "Not surprise, exactly," David said. "Of course, we can't say anything about it. The details won't be released until the morning of the wedding. But it's going to be a magical occasion. We want her to look like a fairy princess."

"We're making six copies of the dress for her," Elizabeth added, "in case of accidents. She can't go out with lipstick smudged on the material, or something like that. But we can't tell you any more. It's virtually a State secret."

They would not even confirm that the wedding dress was to be white. They did say that all their staff had volunteered to sign papers declaring their trustworthiness. Everyone at Emanuel's was determined to keep the details a total secret, and since their trash cans were raided for clues every night, they had even stopped throwing anything away.

Questions about Lady Diana's personality brought more guarded replies. She was wonderful, terribly sweet, and they had adored her the moment they met her.

"I think she'll have a terrific influence on the fashion scene," Elizabeth vouchsafed. "She's young, with a totally fresh approach to fashion, casual but with a great sense of style."

"We were over the moon to be chosen," David added. "It's a very exciting time. But we're frantically busy, as you'll understand, and I'm afraid we'll have to leave it at that."

In the narrow street again, outside the dark blue door that was now firmly closed, Julie added a last few notes to her record of the interview, the page spattered by raindrops, and then went to gaze at the dresses in the window of Emanuel's exclusive small shop. She had to admire the way they had handled all the questions. While talking a lot, they had managed to say nothing new, though what they had said was enough to build an article on.

She trailed back through the rain to the West End and treated herself to a meal in a restaurant overlooking one of the squares, across from the theater she had visited with Hal. From where she sat she could see the posters advertising *Rain Before Seven*, starring Elizabeth Bentham, and she wondered what dark impulse had brought her to that particular place. A miscellany of people came and went along the busy road, dressed in all manner of costume from the conventional to the bizarre, and she saw a scattering of umbrellas that disappeared as the rain stopped.

And then a dark-haired man, tall and of athletic build, came strolling into sight among the crowd. Julie's heart flipped as she recognized Nick, but a second later she was disconcerted to see that he was not alone; a young woman hung on his arm, her curly hair brushing his shoulder as she talked animatedly to him.

Statue-still in her seat, Julie watched as the pair stopped outside the theater to make their farewells. Liz Bentham threw her arms around Nick's neck and kissed him full on the mouth before darting away, though the glass door and into the theater foyer, where she paused to smile and wave. Nick raised a hand in reply, his broad back turned to the window where Julie sat, and she saw him stand for a moment with thumbs hooked into the belt of his jeans before he moved on, becoming lost in the crowd.

Numbness held her immobile, her eyes fixed unseeingly on the spot where he had gone from sight. And what did you expect? she asked herself furiously. You've known it all along. Don't be such a fool, Julie Elliott.

Oddly enough, it didn't hurt. To her surprise she was taking the whole thing with commendable calm. Unnatural calm.

Putting her mind to her work, she took one of the red double deckers down to Hyde Park corner and walked down the long road that followed the high spiked wall around Buckingham Palace gardens. Past some buildings on the corner she came to open gates, where a policeman directed visitors to a door a little further along the wall, where a sign read: Royal Mews, Public Entrance. A small courtyard lay beyond, with a fountain in one corner of a tiny garden area. A line of people waited to pay the entrance fee and have bags checked by a security guard.

Once through the further doors, Julie came in full view of the royal coaches. In the center the fabulous gold state coach, heavily adorned with symbolic gilded figures, glinted dully in the gray light. Beside it stood the other state coaches and the maroon-colored state landau with its double hoods open to display the velvet seats in which the bride and groom would ride back from Saint Paul's if the weather was fine. But the center of attention was the simpler glass coach, light and elegant, its brass lamps gleaming, though Julie was slightly disappointed to see that it was certainly not made of glass. Her brochure explained that the name came from the wide windows of the coach, which would allow the crowds a good view of Lady Diana when she left Clarence House with her father, on her way to meet her bridegroom.

Julie visited the tackrooms full of ornate harnesses and exotic saddles, and the stables where the sleekly groomed bays and the six Windsor grays stood patiently. She interviewed some of the coachmen and grooms, who stood about in frock coats and top hats ready to answer questions or pose for amateur photographers. Although she was fascinated by the treasures of the Royal Mews there seemed to be an ingredient missing from her day. Without Nick . . . no, she mustn't start thinking that way. She had a job to do, and she must concentrate only on that.

Feeling that she had at last attained the right mood of clearheaded efficiency, she spent the evening at International Press preparing articles on everything she had discovered during the previous two days. Her typewriter clacked busily as Jim Dawes appeared and stood by her desk, idly reading through what she had written.

"You met the Spencers?!" he exclaimed. "But everyone's complaining they can't get near them!"

"Well, I did," Julie said. "I thought that was my function." She would have added that her success was due to Nick's magic influence, but to have mentioned his name might have broken down the walls she had carefully erected. Even thinking about him made her head feel as if it might burst.

"Hank's going to be very pleased," the bureau chief told her, still astonished as he stared at her, his gray hair all on end. "He was on the phone earlier, and he said you were doing fine. But this! This is great stuff. And Nick's pictures are superb. This story will probably be syndicated."

She stared at the paper in her typewriter, seeing the words waver. She ought to be pleased with herself, but somehow his compliments seemed unimportant. "Thank you."

"Everything's okay, is it?" Jim Dawes asked with paternal concern. "You seem down, Julie. Why not leave it for tonight? You're well ahead of yourself."

"I'll just finish what I'm doing," she replied.

Aware that he was still hovering, she began to type, her fingers tapping the keys rhythmically. After a while, Jim Dawes took himself away, and Julie, reading what she had just written, tore the sheet from the machine, crumpled it into a tight ball, and tossed it away, missing the wastebasket by a mile. The two other reporters in the office paused momentarily in what they were doing, but she ignored them and grimly fitted another page behind the roller. She intended to get her work up to date, even if it took all night.

A weary Julie returned to the Delphinia well after ten o'clock. Maybe Jim Dawes was right. Maybe she had been overdoing it. Her head ached, and her leg muscles were sore after all the walking she had done lately. London sidewalks were hard on the feet.

"Oh, Miss Elliott," the night porter greeted her as he took her key from its pigeonhole. "Something came for you."

It proved to be a large brown envelope with her name typed on it, but no address and no postage stamp.

"Where did it come from?" she asked.

"It arrived by messenger."

Carrying the envelope, she went up to her room, too tired even to be very curious about the contents of the brown manilla envelope. She flopped onto her bed, wearily kicked off her shoes, and inserted a thumb under the sealed-down flap, tipping the contents onto the bedspread.

Pictures? From Nick?

No, not from Nick. As she saw what they were, a jolt of elation roused her from lethargy—they were snapshots of the young Lady Diana Spencer, exclusive pictures that she had never seen reproduced anywhere before, including one of the royal bride-to-be with another small girl in a treehouse—presumably the one that Michael, the carpenter she had met in Norfolk, had helped to make.

Her heart thumped in her throat as she studied the photographs in disbelief, her hands trembling. Pictures like these were worth a fortune. Together with her interview with the Spencers, they would provide a real scoop!

Except . . .

Except that the only place she had seen pictures like this was in Earl Spencer's treasured albums. Had the earl himself sent them? That was hardly likely, for she had seen how he cherished his family photographs, and if he had wished to publish some more, he would surely have offered them to a British newspaper—and that only with the agreement of Buckingham Palace.

By this time Julie was fully aware of the delicacy of matters surrounding the wedding, and not for anything would she cause offense to the royal family or to the Spencers. Something about the secrecy with which these pictures had been sent to her disturbed her. Suppose they had been stolen?

She needed to discuss the possibilities with someone, and the only person she could think of was Nick. She reached for the phone, but her hand froze in midair as the misery she had been fighting all day rose up to engulf her. She had pretended she didn't care, but the truth was she cared too much, unbearably much. Now the dam burst inside her, and the tears she had kept fiercely in check tore from her in ugly, choking sobs.

A night's sleep helped a little. She woke feeling calmer but empty. Today she would have to see Nick again—it was a problem she had created for herself, and she had to overcome it somehow, in order to get through the seven days before she must fly home.

But if she imagined that Nick was her only problem, she was soon to learn otherwise, for when she came out of the dining room after breakfast and went to hand in her key, the receptionist said, "Oh, Miss Elliott, shall I make up your bill now? You will be out of your room by noon, won't you?"

Julie stared at the woman, wondering which of them was crazy. "Sorry?"

"Your room," came the reply. "We need it for another guest. As a rule, we like people to vacate before noon. If you're worried about your luggage, we can keep that in the baggage room until you want it."

"But I'm booked in until the thirtieth!" Julie exclaimed.

A frown appeared between the receptionist's overplucked brows. "Are you? Let me just check." She leafed through a ledger, checked a box of cards, consulted another book and a computer terminal. "I'm sorry, but you were booked in from Wednesday the fifteenth through Wednesday the twenty-second. Which means you're due to leave today—the twenty-third."

"Then there's been some mistake!" Julie protested. "I'm supposed to be staying here until *next* Thursday. I'm covering the wedding. How can I leave before it's even taken place?"

The receptionist grew more and more tight-lipped as she rechecked but could find no answer to the mystery. Obviously someone had made a mistake, but it was impossible to say whether the culprit was a member of the hotel staff or someone in the office of the *Philadelphia Star*, which had arranged the booking.

"I'm afraid there's not a thing I can do about it," the receptionist said with more sympathy as she recognized the desperation in Julie's face. "Your room has been allocated to someone else starting from today, and all our other rooms are fully booked. I'm afraid you'll have to try somewhere else. Oh, excuse me." Moving away, she picked up the jangling phone, answered it, and gestured at Julie. "It's for you. Will you take it over there, please?"

Feeling as though she were sleepwalking, Julie crossed the deep-pile carpet and picked up the receiver of a phone under a plastic privacy-hood. "Hello?"

"Good morning," came Nick's voice, carefully non-committal. "Are you going to need me today?"

She flung a hand to her head as more tears stung her eyes. "Nick, there's been a mix-up over my hotel booking!" she blurted. "I have to leave the Delphinia today. What am I going to do?"

There was a moment's silence, then he said briskly, "I'll be there as soon as I can."

She waited in one of the comfortable leather seats that were grouped in the foyer, glad that Nick had understood her predicament without need for explanations, though unless he really was a wizard there was probably no way he could help. With the wedding less than a week away, London was overflowing with visitors.

Drifting on a fog of despair, she had no idea how much time passed before she saw Nick stride through the doorway, and then she was so glad to see him that only a last shred of common sense prevented her from hurling herself at him.

"What's all this about?" he asked, a concerned frown on his face.

After Julie had recounted the problem, he went to the desk and demanded explanations from the receptionist, for whom Julie had only sympathy. The mix-up wasn't the woman's fault, but she felt the full force of Nick's temper before he returned to sit by Julie, his face taut.

"Don't worry, we'll find you something."

She lost count of the phone calls they made and the amount of small change that was swallowed by the machine, with Nick growing less sanguine as each hotel they called gave the same answer—fully booked until after the twenty-ninth.

"I can always sleep on Maddie's couch, if she'll have me," Julie said, sighing. "I'll call her. Have you got another five-pence piece?"

He held up the coin between finger and thumb. "Just one left."

"Thank you."

Maddie Venables was her last hope. Knowing she had a lot of nerve even asking, Julie put the question to her new-found friend, only to have Maddie say with real regret that her flatmate's two cousins had already moved in to the basement to stay for the wedding, so the place was overcrowded as it was.

"I'm ever so sorry, Julie," she concluded. "Any other time you'd have been welcome. But I'm sure you'll find somewhere."

"Yes, of course I will," Julie replied with a certainty she did not feel. "It was just a thought. Thanks, Maddie."

She ducked out of the privacy hood to see Nick lift his eyebrows in a query to which she shook her head. "I'll have to bed down at the office. Or on the embankment."

Seven

Feeling as though she were trapped in some weird, nonsensical dream, Julie followed Nick into the foyer of a sumptuous apartment building, where he introduced her to the uniformed doorman as, "Miss Julie Elliott. She'll be staying with me for a few days, Trimble."

"Very good, sir," the man replied with no change of expression as he touched the braided peak of his cap.

An elevator door slid open for them, and Julie stepped into the paneled interior, catching sight of her flushed reflection in a big mirror. Everything about the place was polished, with an air of opulence that bewildered her, but she made no comment as Nick pressed the top button and they were lifted smoothly to a small hallway containing two doors, one of which he unlocked.

He ushered her into the main room of his apartment. Black leather furniture reposed on a tan carpet, with glass tables shining in the light that poured through a huge window. Julie glimpsed a view of greenery that must be Kensington Gardens, with the buildings of London in the distance and a skyscape of scurrying clouds. Striped curtains framed the window, and to one side was a dining bar with four stools.

The kitchen area beyond gleamed with stainless steel fittings. But what might have been a functional, severely masculine room was softened by various plants set in ceramic pots and by the framed blowups of photographs that hung on the walls—studies of dancers, old people, and children. The apartment was spacious, elegant, and, Julie thought, must be very expensive.

"You live here?" she asked in disbelief.

"Yes," he said briefly, crossing to a further doorway. "Your room's through here. If you'd like to get settled in, I'll make us some coffee."

More photographs adorned the walls of the inner hallway, from where Nick led her into a twin-bedded room with fitted wardrobes and a long dressing table set beneath a wide mirror.

"Make yourself at home," he said, dumping her luggage on the floor before departing without a glance at her.

Swallowing hard, Julie went to the window and looked down to the street far below, where a few cars were parked in the front courtyard of the apartment building. She had imagined that Nick's apartment would not be so different from Maddie's, but it was a penthouse. And she was to stay here, alone with him.

Oh, she couldn't! It was a crazy idea.

She turned to the door, wanting to go out and tell him she couldn't possibly stay, but he was already irritated. He would ask what alternative she had, and really there was no alternative.

Knowing that she was taking a risk, Julie decided to treat the whole thing the way Nick was treating it—as an inconvenient answer to her problem. After all, it was only for seven nights, and if she kept her cool there should be no trouble. She opened her suitcase and began to take out her belongings.

As she opened the wardrobe she paused, her heart jerking uncomfortably at the sight of a woman's coat hanging there, with two pairs of high-heeled shoes set neatly on the floor. She felt very much the interloper as she placed her own clothes in the cupboard and opened the top drawer of the chest to be confronted by filmy underwear—obviously left there in case the owner found herself staying overnight unexpectedly. She had no need to wonder who the clothes belonged to. She knew very well which woman must stay with Nick when the occasion suited.

Oh, damn! She pressed her fingertips hard against her forehead in an effort to stop the jealous thoughts. He was a normal, virile man. Why should it bother her that Liz Bentham sometimes stayed with him? She had guessed it would be so. She had known it. But to have it blatantly thrown in her face this way was too much to bear. Was it Nick's way of reminding her that he was unavailable?

More feminine accoutrements were set on the bathroom shelves, including a bottle of luxury bath oil and a box of dusting powder, but by that time the message had gone home, and Julie was beyond surprise. To have mentioned the items would only have embarrassed both herself and Nick, so she decided to pretend she had noticed nothing unusual.

"Is the room all right?" he asked as she returned to the sitting room.

"It's fine, thanks. I'll try not to be more of a nuisance than I have to be." Holding herself in check against the trembling that had seized her, she sank down onto one of the big leather armchairs. "I needn't be here too much. During the day we'll be out, and I'll need to be at IP to do my write-ups in the evenings, so I won't be in your way."

He poured two cups of coffee from a percolator on the bar and brought them to the low glass table in front of her, setting them carefully down before straightening himself, frowning down at her. "There's no need to go to extremes. I'm not an animal."

"That wasn't what—"she began, turning hot and cold as she let her eyes meet his and saw the bitterness there. Looking at his middle shirt button, she went on, "You did say it would be inconvenient for you. I was just trying to make it easier."

"I know." Sighing, he lowered his tall frame into

another chair and leaned on his knees. "Listen, Julie. . . . The other night, I—I don't know what got into me. Can we forget about that?"

"I can if you can," she said lightly, reaching for her coffee so that she could avoid his glance. "I asked for it, I guess. I was developing a silly crush on you, and I let it show, but you've cured me of that. We're working colleagues, that's all. From now on, I'll remember it."

She sipped at the coffee, which burned her throat as it went down, but the pain was welcome at that moment—it gave her something to think about other than dwelling on the muscular man who sat not many feet away. Those strong hands had touched and held her, and she still remembered how his kisses had felt. Forget it? Dear heaven, how could she?

He made no reply to her flippant admission, and the silence lengthened between them, vibrating painfully along her nerves. What was he thinking? She didn't dare look up to try to read his expression in case her own face showed more than she cared for him to know, but she was fairly sure that he would guess nothing from her demeanor. To outward appearances she was relaxed and indifferent, and she would be careful to keep up that front.

"What have you got planned for today?" he asked eventually.

That was a safe subject, thank goodness. "I thought I might have another try at meeting some of the other youngsters who are going to be Lady Diana's attendants. And I'd like to inverview Bill Pashley, if I can. He's making the going-away outfit, so I understand, and he often makes clothes for Lady Diana. He sounds like quite a character."

"Does he? I can't say I know much about him, apart from his name, but then I'm not as passionately interested as you are. Did you happen to be around Saint Paul's when everyone arrived for the wedding rehearsal yesterday?"

"No, I missed that. But I did see Lady Diana at the Emanuels'."

"By chance?"

"Well, yes." Keeping her face carefully under control and trying not to remember who else she had seen by chance the previous day, she lifted her head. "Apparently Hank Freeman's very pleased with what we've done so far. Mr. Dawes told me so last night. He was especially impressed by that interview with the Spencers. I really have to thank you for that. But something odd happened when I got back last night." A frown creased her brow as she recalled the incident. "Someone had sent me some photographs—of Lady Diana when she was young. I've no idea where they came from, so I'm in two minds about the wisdom of giving them to Jim Dawes for publication."

"Oh? Why?"

"In case whoever sent them got hold of them illegally."

Nick regarded her without expression. "That's not very likely, is it? If they'd been stolen, the thief would have demanded a large sum of money from one of the big papers or from television. Or was there a bill with them?"

"A bill?"

"A check—a statement of account."

"No," she said, shaking her head. "Just the pictures. You don't suppose that Earl Spencer . . . surely not! But I can't think of anyone else. Do you think it would be okay to publish them?"

"Why not?" he replied, shrugging. "If something like that falls into your lap, make use of it. I didn't know American journalists had that many scruples."

"Some of us do," Julie said. "Anyhow, if you think it will be okay, I'll take them in to the office as soon as possible. They're a real scoop. Hank Freeman will never believe it. He'll probably promote me because of this!"

Her voice sounded falsely bright, echoing in the emptiness inside her, and she hardly noticed that Nick failed to react. He was watching her thoughtfully, a little frown making a line down his forehead beneath the tumble of dark hair.

"Is that where you were last night—at the office? Until after ten?"

"There was a lot to catch up on."

His mouth twisted, and he looked down at the hands clasped between his knees. "I phoned you three times to try and apologize. When it got to be so late, I thought . . ." A sharp laugh escaped him, and he leaned back in the chair, throwing out a hand. "I thought you'd gone out with Hal, just to spite me."

Bewilderment washed over her, sending a peculiar prickle down her spine. What a strange thing for him to say. "To spite you? I don't follow."

"No, neither do I," he said, and pushed himself out of the chair. "We'd better be getting on with some work. Get your coat and let's go."

During the rest of the day he seemed distant, much as he had been when they first met. They managed to accomplish nearly everything Julie had hoped for—except that, as usual, no one was prepared to break the secrecy surrounding wedding details.

That evening she returned to the office alone. Fortunately Maddie Venables had by that time finished work, which saved Julie from having to explain that she had found accommodations in Nick's apartment. She settled down to work, delaying as long as she could because the thought of going back to her new lodgings made her nervous. Nick's aloofness during the day had helped her keep her own feelings in check, but when they were alone again, everything might change.

Eventually, however, she had no alternative but to make her way across the city to Wellesley Court.

As she stepped out of the elevator, the door of Nick's apartment opened and he appeared there, a glass in one hand, his shirt half open and his hair disheveled.

"It's not safe for you to be out alone so late," he said. "Why didn't you call? I'd have come and picked you up."

"There was no need to trouble yourself," she replied, walking swiftly past him. Only one lamp was turned on, shedding a bright glow over a table in the corner, where papers spilled in an untidy heap; the rest of the room lay in shadow. "Have you been working, too?"

"Got to catch up on my paperwork some time," he said, his voice coming from close behind her as he closed the door. "I didn't realize how late it was until I got up just now to pour myself a drink, and then I started worrying. London isn't as bad as New York, but it's still not safe for a woman on her own after dark. Another time, I'll fetch you in the car. Would you like a drink?"

Glancing over her shoulder, she saw him as a tall shape in the dimness, close enough to touch. She moved away. "No, thank you. I'm so tired I'll get straight to bed. Don't work too late. Good night."

If he replied it was so low that she didn't hear it. She made for the inner hall and put its door between them, congratulating herself on having conquered the worst hurdle.

Somehow the two of them coped with the early morning, each giving the other a wide berth until they met over breakfast in the slate-gray light of morning. Gazing down on the rain-glazed trees and pathways of Kensington Gardens, Julie mourned that it was more like fall than summer, with a cold wind sending flurries of drops to spatter the big window.

She and Nick talked about the weather and of the day ahead, both avoiding any personal topics. It was, she thought, like tiptoeing across a minefield to which they had a map, picking a way one step at a time, sometimes drawing back from the edge of disaster and sometimes forging swiftly ahead across safe ground, but the field was endless, and the mines remained a constant threat. She kept assuring herself that only *she* was aware of the undercurrents, but every so often Nick stopped short in the middle of a sentence that might have led him astray, or she caught a fleeting look in his eye that told her he was as sensitive as she was to the things they were avoiding putting into words.

That Friday morning London seemed to have taken on an extra surge of excitement. Red, white, and blue decorations proliferated everywhere, with pictures of the royal couple and Union Jacks intermingled with flowers in the wedding colors of silver, pink, and purple. Julie even caught a glimpse of the soldiers returning to their Knightsbridge barracks after full-dress rehearsals in Hyde Park. Despite the weather they made a fine sight, red plumes bobbing over helmets and cuirasses polished to a mirror sheen, their horses groomed to silky perfection.

During the afternoon, when the rain let up a little, she and Nick found themselves near Hyde Park, where they bought coffee from a refreshment booth and sat on one of the benches beneath trees that rustled in the wind. Not far away the Serpentine ruffled its waters beneath a gray sky, babies and dogs were being walked, a couple of children kicked a ball, and people strolled across the wet grass.

"If it had been a good day," Nick said, "this place would be full of sunbathers."

Julie shivered. "Not much chance of that this summer. I'll stay wrapped up, thank you."

"You usually do," he commented. "Do you realize I've never seen you in anything but trousers?"

"Pants are my usual working gear," she replied.

He got up to toss his cardboard cup into a litter bin and, seeming restless, picked up his camera and strolled away, snapping some of the passersby while Julie watched him, her green eyes clouded with sadness. Look at him now—crouching to take a picture of a baby in a stroller while the proud mother preened, flattered by his interest, responding as most women did to the attractive cameraman with the strong frame and handsome face. Julie's teeth ached with hopeless jealousy. He seemed able to talk to anyone with easy charm—anyone except her. Why was she the exception? He was friendly and smiling—with Maddie Venables, with each passing stranger, but every time he came back to Julie a guard came down across his expression.

She saw it happen again as he strolled back toward her, rewinding the film in his camera: a veil dropped over his eyes, as if he were wary of her, or uncertain.

"I'm out of film," he said, resuming his seat on the bench to put his camera away in its case. "I must buy some more. By the way, have you got an evening dress with you?"

"At the apartment, you mean?" she asked, knotting her brow. "No, I didn't bother bringing one. Why?"

"I just wondered." Snapping the lock of the case, he looked directly at her, still wearing that unreadable mask. "You could buy one, I suppose. You see . . . we've been invited to a party tomorrow night."

"*We* have?"

"That's right. I'm sure you'll enjoy it, meeting my friends and so forth. Their place is out in the country, so we'll be staying over Saturday night."

"When was this arranged?" she asked.

"The party's been planned for months, but I've made sure they know I'm bringing you. They're looking forward to meeting you."

She didn't understand him. Wouldn't Liz object to his taking another woman to an overnight party?

"I really don't think it would be a very good idea, Nick."

His mouth tightened in a way she had come to recognize as a warning sign that his temper was rising. "Don't be so prim and proper! I've gone out of my way to arrange for you to go. They'll have a room ready for you—a single room, in case you're wondering. If I ring and say you're not coming after all, they'll think I've gone potty."

"Then you should have asked me first!" she returned. "Besides, I want to stay in London this weekend. Prince Charles is due to play polo at Windsor on Sunday. I want to be there to see him."

"You and every other journalist!" he exclaimed. "With all the VIPs there, not to mention the TV crews, it will be a stampede. You won't get anywhere near the prince."

"But I want to try! It may be my only chance."

"All right, suppose I promise to get you back in time

for the polo match. What other excuse can you come up with?"

His insistence puzzled her, but she was even more bothered by the voice inside her that was urging her to accept, to spend a weekend in the country with him and to buy a dress that would make him forget Liz Bentham. The temptation was enormous.

But before she could form any sort of reply, a commotion along the path drew their attention to a little boy who was being pestered by a pair of large and noisy dogs. The animals leaped and prowled around the child, who made ineffectual gestures at them as he backed away, being herded toward the bench where Nick and Julie sat.

Cursing, Nick sprang to his feet and strode toward the child, sweeping him off the ground. The dogs crouched menacingly for a second, then as Nick took a determined step toward them, they whirled and ran off among the trees.

"Is he okay?" Julie asked, peering at the fair head pressed into Nick's shoulder. Great tears welled in the boy's eyes and plopped down grubby cheeks. "Poor lamb, he's scared to death."

"Somebody ought to take a whip to people who let their dogs roam like that," Nick growled, cradling the child against his chest and stroking the fair curls with a big, gentle hand.

"What's your name, honey?" Julie asked the child.

Sniffling, he said his name was Timmie Weston and he had lost his mummy.

"Well, you're safe now," Nick said softly. "We'll find your mummy for you. Think you can walk? It's okay, the dogs have gone."

Bending, he set the child on his feet and told him to hold Julie's hand. Then he collected his camera case, and with the child between them they set off along the path, Nick talking quietly and cheerfully. Timmie soon forgot his fright and began to reply to Nick's questions, while Julie listened, her throat tight with emotion. This was another side of Nick—a gentle, caring side that she had only glimpsed before. What a great father he would make, and how fortunate the woman who was mother to his children.

No, she mustn't think like that! She squeezed her eyes shut, shaking away the daydreams. What was the point of dreaming things that couldn't ever come true?

When she opened her eyes again, she saw a distraught woman running along the path toward them, calling, "Timmie! Oh, Timmie!"

"Mummy!" the child cried, and rushed away to be enveloped in his mother's arms while she wept with relief. She mumbled incoherent thanks as Nick explained what had happened, then she hurried away with Timmie holding tightly to her hand.

"That's one story with a happy ending, anyway," Nick said, smiling. "Nice piece of human interest for you, if you're short of copy."

"Yes." She mirrored his smile, their differences momentarily forgotten. "You were wonderful with him, Nick. It's marvelous the way people respond to you."

To her dismay she saw the barrier go up again, though what she had said to cause it she couldn't think. "It must be that charisma you were talking about the other day," he said. "Pity it doesn't have a universal effect. Well, what about that party? Will you come? You've been working like a slave these last few days. Give yourself some time off. You might regret it if you don't."

She would probably regret it if she did, but six days from now she would be back in the States, and if she had made a fool of herself, no one would know it except her.

"Just so long as we're back for that polo match," she replied, mentally crossing her fingers for luck. "I've promised myself a close view of Prince Charles before I leave."

Soon after that they parted, Nick to buy his film and Julie to scour the fashion shops for a dress suitable for a buffet-dance at a country house. It took her the rest of the afternoon, but eventually she found the very dress she wanted, a floaty affair made of layers of flame-colored chiffon. Somehow she hoped that the weekend might work some kind of miracle. The dreams were growing too strong to be ignored.

Later, she returned to the IP office along a Fleet Street now gay with fluttering bunting. She had almost finished her articles for that day when, to her surprise, Nick arrived, come to escort her back to Wellesley Court.

"I've left a casserole simmering," he told her. "You're probably just as sick of restaurant meals as I am, so I thought we'd eat at home tonight—if you have no objections."

Dark lashes veiled his eyes, as if he suspected she might argue. *Eat at home.* How intimate it sounded. Smiling brightly, Julie said she would enjoy sampling his cooking. "I had no idea you were so domesticated."

"Yes, well . . ." he said under his breath. "There's a lot you don't know about me yet. Just finish what you're doing. I'll wait."

We can be adult about it, he had said before she moved into his apartment, and she was trying—oh, how she was trying! But it wasn't so easy when her senses were constantly alert to him. His voice made dark music, his clean masculine odor had become too familiar, his lightest touch started fireworks inside her, and even the sight of him had the power to make her heart quicken.

On the way back to Kensington, sitting beside him in the MG, she talked too much, saying the most inane things and inwardly cursing herself for behaving just like the ingenuous child he thought her. Nick himself seemed grave, replying to her breathless chatter in calm, deep monosyllables, though his eyes held a subtle reproach that stung her.

As soon as they reached the penthouse, she escaped to the bathroom, hoping that a cool wash might calm her. Being with Nick had become sweet torture, but perhaps she was a masochist, for she would rather be with him than without him. She had never known that emotions could be so confusing.

Remembering his remark about never seeing her in anything but pants, she was woman enough to toy with the idea of putting on a skirt, though she discarded the thought immediately. Darn it, she was supposed to be playing it safe, not going out of her way to attract him. So she stayed as she was, in blue jeans and a cheesecloth shirt, though she brushed out her hair and smudged a fresh touch of color on her lips for the sake of her morale.

Thankfully, she discovered the living room ablaze with light—soft lighting would have been much too intimate for this occasion, and presumably Nick had known it. He, too, was playing it safe, reminding her in many subtle ways that she was staying with him only as a matter of convenience.

They sat opposite each other at the dining bar, eating the aromatic chicken casserole he had prepared and drinking a dry white wine chilled in an ice bucket. For a while they ate in silence, until Julie's nerves clamored for something to ease the tension.

"Do you rent this apartment?" she asked.

"In a way," he replied. "I have an understanding with the owner. He's not here very often, so he lets me live here."

"I see. I did kind of wonder how you afforded it. I mean—" She stopped herself as his eyebrow raised sardonically.

"I do fairly well for myself, you know," he said quietly.

"Oh, I'm sure you do. I didn't mean. . . . I was just making conversation."

"I'm aware of that. This flat's ideal for me, as it happens. It has its own studio."

Surprised, she glanced around the room. "It does? Where?"

"Upstairs," he said with a gesture at the ceiling. "I'll show it to you after dinner, if you're interested."

"Fine!" Anything to fill in time until she could

escape to her room without making it obvious she was avoiding him.

He poured more wine from the bottle, refilling her glass. Looking askance at the pale liquid, she wondered if she ought to drink any more. Wine went straight to her head, but it did have the advantage of relaxing her, so perhaps the benefits outweighed the risks, as long as she didn't overdo it.

By the time Nick set the empty bottle upside-down in the ice bucket, she had begun to feel slightly euphoric and sentimental. Here she was alone with the man she adored, with only a few days remaining of her dream trip to England. What harm could it do if she indulged in a secret, unrequited love, even if she paid for it with pain and remorse?

"Come and see the studio," Nick suggested, easing himself to his feet.

She followed him across the room, free for once to gaze at him without his being aware of her scrutiny. Her fingers itched to tangle again in the hair that curled at his neck, and to smooth the broad shoulders beneath that slightly crumpled shirt. She wished she did not know how it felt to be held in his arms, for the memory only made her want to renew the feeling.

In the outer hall he unlocked the mysterious second door, which she had assumed must lead to another apartment. Now, as Nick snapped on a light, she saw a flight of stairs leading upward.

"Secret passages, even," she said lightly as she followed him up the stairs. "Is this where you keep your etchings?"

Only as he glanced around to give her a sharp look did she realize what an idiotic remark it had been.

"Sorry," she muttered. "Bad joke."

A door at the top of the stairs opened into a big room that lay in darkness except for the lights of London spread out beyond a window that filled one wall. The glow showed her the shape of big lamps on leggy stands and a few pieces of furniture, around which she made her way to the window as if mesmerized. Below,

117

yellow lamps were strung across Kensington Gardens, leading her eye to the interwoven necklaces of lights in the distance, a panorama that glittered in the darkness like a piece of fairyland.

"It's beautiful!" she exclaimed. "London by night. . . . Don't you think it's the most exciting place in the world?"

"How much of the world have you seen?" he asked with gentle mockery, his voice floating across the room behind her. "But you're right—it is quite something."

"Quite something?" Laughing breathlessly, she turned to face him, but her eyes were so full of the lights that in the darkness he was invisible. "I'd heard the British have a talent for understatement, but that's the most ..." The words trailed off as she strained to see where he was. "Nick?"

"I'm here," he said from somewhere to her right, and she heard a swish as long drapes began to spread across the window, shutting out the view—shutting out every trace of light.

She stood still, her heart thumping madly, and her head swimming from the effects of the wine. What was he planning to do? Searching wildly for some trace of normality, she managed another unsteady laugh. "What's this, your darkroom?"

"No, the darkroom's next door." He sounded to be coming toward her through the impenetrable blackness, and panic beat at her in suffocating waves.

"Don't bother to show me that," she blurted. "This place is dark enough for me. What do you work with—infra-red? Or by sense of touch?"

With a click, soft light flooded the room from concealed lamps along the ceiling. Nick stood by the door, a bleak look on his face. "Is that another bad joke?"

"Sorry. My timing's lousy tonight. Darkness always makes me nervous."

"You've been nervous since you first stepped into my flat," he observed.

Wishing she could keep her stupid mouth shut, she turned away to look around the room, seeing the reflecting screens and the big spotlights on spindly stands. On a dais in a corner stood a low couch backed by black curtains designed to be drawn around a dressing area that boasted a large mirror. A door in the side wall obviously led into the darkroom where Nick processed his film.

"It's very—businesslike," she said.

"What did you expect?" he demanded harshly. "A kingsize bed and mirrors on the ceiling?"

"Of course not!"

"Then why do you keep implying that I use this place for seduction?"

"I don't!" She flung a hand to her head, turning her back to him. "I can't think straight. You shouldn't have given me so much wine."

"Meaning I gave it to you intentionally?" he asked, his voice low and ominous.

Taking a deep breath, she whirled to face him, swaying momentarily as giddiness made her head reel. "You might have."

"Thank you!"

He looked as though he would have liked to throttle her, she thought wildly. Trapped in a situation of her own making, she could only respond with anger of her own. "Well, why did you bring me up here? Why pull the drapes before you put the light on? It's not as if anyone could see in. You were deliberately trying to unsettle me."

"You get unsettled every time I come within five feet of you," he growled, suddenly striding toward her.

Trying to avoid him, she turned aside, her shoulder catching one of the lamps. She grabbed for it, and Nick lunged forward. Between them they saved the lamp from smashing to disaster, but somehow one of her hands became trapped beneath his on the metal stand, and she froze, staring into brown eyes that snapped with temper.

"Just be a bit more careful," he said. "These things are expensive."

"You frightened me!" she exclaimed, her skin vibrating beneath the warmth of his hand. "Starting toward me like that. I didn't know what you were going to do. I never know what you're going to do next."

"Ditto!" he retorted furiously. "First it's the green light, then it's the cold shoulder. I don't know where the hell I am with you. I'm not made of wood, you know."

Although he was holding her only lightly, she was powerless to move away and break that contact. Her senses spun in the knowledge of his nearness as she stared up into his frowning face, seeing it shimmer through sudden hot tears.

"I don't understand you," she choked.

"I thought I was making myself abysmally clear," he said bitterly.

"I mean I haven't understood a thing you've said or done since the night we met! You're the one who blows hot and cold. You get angry for no reason at all. You stop talking to me, and I never know why. And then suddenly you'll make fun of me. I've never known anyone with so many moods, and I don't understand any of them."

He moved swiftly away from the lamp, lifting his hands to cup her face, his thumbs brushing the tears from her cheeks. "It took me a long time to understand myself," he said in an undertone. "Don't let me upset you, please. You're not really afraid of me, are you?"

Trembling, she shook her head, too choked up to speak. Of course she wasn't afraid of him. Perhaps she was afraid of the effect he had on her, but not of Nick himself. She loved him, and at that moment she didn't care if it showed on her face or in the quivering of her fingers as they rested against his shirt. She had thrown her hand there to keep him away, but it was strangely helpless now as her nerve ends explored the softness of cotton material over warm muscle.

Very slowly he bent toward her, his eyes turning almost black as he searched her face before letting his lips meet hers tentatively, asking silent questions. Unable to help herself, she swayed toward him in instinctive invitation, guilty pleasure shivering through her as he took her tightly in his arms.

Time ceased to exist. She forgot about Liz Bentham, about the Philadelphia Elliotts, about everything but the sheer joy of being held so close to this special man. Everything in her was alive to him: her fingers explored the texture of his hair and the warm strength of his shoulders. Her only desire was to have him continue holding her, caressing her, both of them swept up in a passionate longing for each other.

She felt his fingers warm on her midriff, where her shirt had parted from her belt, moving almost shyly across the softness of her flesh to cup her breast through silky lace, and an uncontrollable shudder ran through her.

He became still, lifting his head to look down into her flushed face, at drowsy green eyes and passion-softened lips, then gently withdrew his hand from beneath her shirt before pressing her head to his shoulder.

With his arms tightly about her and his cheek resting on her hair, Julie stared unseeingly across the softly lit room, becoming aware of the world again. Her face burned, and she couldn't bear to look at him. She remained leaning on him, her cheek pressed to the warm skin at the base of his throat, while beneath her ear his heart beat a pagan tattoo.

"Forgive me," he said hoarsely. "I swore I wouldn't even touch you."

"And I swore I wouldn't let you," she choked, closing her eyes against searing-hot tears.

Sighing heavily, he released his hold on her, letting his fingers slide through her hair, to her shoulders, and down her arms, to catch her hands in his. "We mustn't let it happen again," he said. "It's much too dangerous."

"I know." Unable to face him, she stared at the point in his throat where a pulse jumped visibly beneath his skin.

"Maybe you'd better get to bed," he suggested softly. "I'll stay up here for a while."

"Okay."

But neither of them moved, their hands laced tightly

121

together, though who was holding whom was not clear. At last she found the courage to lift her eyes to his and discovered him watching her with a regret that matched her own. "Nick—"

"Shh," he breathed, then leaned to taste her lips one last tender time. "Don't say anything. Not now. Good night."

In the sanctuary of her room she leaned against the door, breathing heavily as if she had been running. Nothing in her experience had prepared her for the way Nick had made her feel. She had been ready to do whatever he wanted, and it hadn't seemed wrong, not at the time. But now she could only be thankful that he had had the sense to call a halt, even though his reasons for doing so tore her apart.

He, at least, remembered in time that for him the attraction was merely physical. He was being faithful to Liz Bentham.

Eight

By the time she woke, Nick had gone out, leaving a note to say that he would return in time for an early lunch, since he planned to set out for the country by one o'clock. She guessed that he had left the apartment in order to avoid her company, but she couldn't object to that. The previous night's encounter had been too shattering for her to have faced him without time to get the thing into perspective. Presumably he felt the same.

She treated herself to a long soak in the bath, washed her hair, and indulged in a full beauty treatment, with half her mind on the party that evening, even though she was fairly sure she would not be going. It would be a shame to waste that gorgeous gown she had bought, but she had to be sensible, and it seemed safest of all for her to stay in London while Nick went to his friends' house for the weekend. With miles between them there could be no danger.

Sitting wrapped in a towel with her hair slowly drying naturally, she applied a last coat of polish to her nails, feeling clean and fresh all over. And that was when she heard a door bang and Nick's voice come from the inner hallway, calling her name.

"I'm in here!" she replied, anxious eyes on the door handle.

"I'm going to make a start on lunch," he informed her. "Steak and salad suit you?"

"Yes, fine." She breathed freely again as she heard him return to the main room, though she was irritated with herself. What had she expected him to do, for heaven's sake? Walk uninvited into her bedroom? Nick wasn't like that.

Allowing the polish plenty of time to dry, she dressed in her white slacks and red shirt, brushed out her hair, and took a few deep, calming breaths before walking boldly out to join Nick in the kitchen area.

"Anything I can do?"

He was turning the steaks under the grill, where they sizzled and sent out an appetizing aroma. "Yes, you can toss the salad, if you like. There's some French dressing in that top cupboard."

"It smells good," she said, having to pass close to him to reach the cupboard, which made Nick pause in what he was doing and look at her for the first time.

"So do you," was all he said in words, but in his eyes there was a questioning light that told her he had not forgotten the previous night.

"I've had a bath." She grabbed the bottle of dressing and retreated to the bar, where the bowl of salad stood waiting. Shaking the oil and vinegar over it, she began to turn the vegetables with wooden servers, her hands none too steady. It was ridiculous that she should shake so just because he stood within touching distance, watching her.

"Nick . . ." The salad would have to do; she couldn't concentrate. She set down the servers and stared at the little blobs of oil she had spattered on the heat-proof surface of the bar. "I really don't think it's a good idea for me to go with you today."

"Why not?" he asked.

"You know why not. Don't be obtuse."

"There's no good reason why you shouldn't come," he said. "There'll be plenty of other people around—a houseful of them. We needn't be alone for a minute. Unless we want to be."

She made herself face him, filled with a sense of regret. "That's the problem, isn't it?"

"It needn't be a problem unless we allow it to be," he replied quietly, his eyes steady on hers. "You need to relax a bit. Next week you'll be chasing about doing the final build-up and then covering the wedding itself. I know you're keen to do a good job to impress your editor, but you don't have to work yourself into the ground, do you? How much socializing have you done since you arrived here—apart from going to the theater with Hal Greaves?"

Something in his voice as he mentioned Hal's name made Julie wince. "I spent an evening with Maddie Venables, too," she said defensively.

"That was a week ago. You need another break. It will only be for twenty-four hours. Please, come with me."

Responding to the earnest plea in his eyes, Julie took a deep breath and capitulated, suddenly aware of how time was passing. Five days from now she would be on her way back to the States, and everything would be over. Everything.

She didn't have much appetite, but she applied herself to the meal with stubborn desperation, all the time aware of Nick sitting beside her, his shirt-sleeves rolled up to display bronzed forearms covered in a light growth of dark hair.

At least the weather had improved, she thought, forcing her mind into safer channels. The wind appeared to have veered, chasing away most of the clouds to let the sun shine through, and in the park below, people wore light summer clothes, so the day must be quite warm.

"Talking about last Saturday," Nick said after a while. "When you told me you were going out to dinner, I assumed you meant you had another date with Hal. I tried phoning you later on, but you weren't there, and when I called again and they said you had been out all night, I'm afraid I jumped to conclusions. So if I was foul to you, that's why."

She saw that he had become very still, empty fork poised over his plate. "Is that what you were apologizing about—when we came back from Chatham?" she asked, so tense that her breathing came fast and shallow.

"Yes, I'm afraid so." He gave her a shamefaced glance. "You wouldn't believe the times I've cursed myself for taking you to the Cheshire Cheese that first day. If I'd known Hal was going to be there, I'd have avoided the place like the plague."

"Because you were afraid I couldn't cope with a vile seducer?"

He laid down his fork and pushed his plate away. "If you believe that you'll believe anything," he said, and got to his feet. "I'll just clear up here, and then we'll be off. Have you got your overnight bag packed?"

"No."

"Then go and do it. Time's getting on."

Leaving her seat, she made for the inner hall, too cowardly to ask what he had meant by that enigmatic remark about Hal. Did he mean that he had been jealous?

As Nick looked at her expectantly she shrugged and moved out of his sight, telling herself that she must be imagining things again.

Having little idea of the geography of England, Julie didn't ask exactly where they were heading but settled back into the red leather seat to enjoy the views as the MG rushed along a highway, escaping the choking traffic of the city. Nick pointed out the ramparts of Windsor Castle as they swept by and came off the highway onto a road that seemed to be following the course of the Thames; every few minutes Julie glimpsed water glinting in the sunlight, often with boats sailing on it.

By mid-afternoon they had come to rolling uplands, which Nick said were the Berkshire Downs. He was driving more slowly, along narrow winding lanes that dipped and rose across the contours of the countryside, first in a valley full of trees and now reaching a crest that gave a wide view of wooded hills and grassy sweeps of land, with farms and villages nestling in the hollows.

"This is why I wanted to start in good time," he told her, "so I could show you something of the countryside. Or is it too bucolic for your taste?"

"It's heavenly," she said, meaning it. "I'm glad you made me come. I did need a break, I guess. You, too."

"We both needed a change of scene," Nick replied gravely, and they exchanged an eloquent look that had nothing to do with their banal conversation.

At length they came down a tree-cloaked slope that wound into a broad valley where Julie glimpsed another village, with, on its outskirts, a big house half-hidden behind yet more trees. On an open grassy field in the valley bottom, figures in white stood about, apparently involved in a game of cricket, while spectators lazed under the trees.

"It's years since I watched a cricket match," Nick said. "Do you mind if we stop for a while?"

"No, not at all, if we have time."

"All the time in the world," he assured her.

He turned down a narrow lane beneath chestnut trees whose big leaves danced in the sunlight. The way appeared to be barred by a block of buildings over a central archway, but Nick drove straight beneath the arch and on between meadows dotted with trees, over a small bridge that crossed a stream. Before them lay the big house, a grand mansion of honey-colored stone with a castellated roof and leaded windows winking between swathes of roses. It was set against the slope of the further hill, above terraced gardens where gentle flights of steps led up between stone urns brilliant with flowers. Below the gardens the lane twisted, one branch running up behind the house while the other led to the cricket field. Cars were parked beneath trees near the stream.

Glad to stretch her legs, Julie climbed from the car

and followed Nick's lithe figure beneath the bowed branches of an ancient oak tree, beyond which the spectators formed a rough circle perhaps a hundred yards across. Families sat in the shade, with picnic baskets that overflowed. By a tent on which was a sign, Refreshments, several dozen deck chairs had been set, and most of them were occupied by reclining forms.

"Howzat?!" went up the shout from the field, and a spatter of applause came from the watching circle.

"Nothing quite like it on a lazy summer's afternoon," Nick said. "Would you like a drink?"

They found two spare deck chairs and sat sipping tea from cardboard cups while he explained what was happening on the field. Julie found herself confused by the intricacies of the game and references to such things as "square leg" and "silly mid-on," which apparently were positions on the field.

Her eyes on the incomprehensible movements of the white-clad figures, she puzzled over the change that had come over Nick. He had been in a hurry to leave London, yet now he seemed content to sit and watch this leisurely game, though she would have sworn that he was not as relaxed as he seemed.

"Do you mind if I take a walk?" she asked.

"No, go ahead. But don't be long. I don't intend to stay here all afternoon."

"Do we have much farther to go?"

"Only up the road." He gave her a rueful grimace. "Actually, Julie. . . . No, it doesn't matter. I'll tell you when you get back."

Frowning to herself, she walked back toward the lane. She would never understand that man, she thought for the hundredth time. It was almost as if he were reluctant to arrive wherever he was going.

With a clatter of wings, a pigeon took flight from a tree nearby to swoop across the terraces in front of the big old house. Julie paused in the shade, staring up at the battlemented walls and rose-clung facade, wondering how long the place had stood there. Hundreds of years, at a guess, being altered and added to until it attained its present state of pleasing asymmetry. It was, she thought, the most beautiful house she had ever seen.

Finding herself unable to stay away from Nick for very long, she turned back toward the cricket field hoping that he might tell her what he was up to this time. She had begun to feel jittery about the forthcoming meeting with his friends.

It was no help when she saw that her deck chair had been claimed by a young woman who was talking to Nick as if she had known him for years. A big-brimmed straw hat protected her face from the sun, and a flimsy summer dress with long sleeves was draped elegantly against her figure. Pausing for a second, Julie thought darkly that here was yet another woman who had responded to Nick on sight, but this time she wasn't going to stand by and watch it happen. She strode on purposefully, feeling evil.

As she approached the pair, Nick caught sight of her and stood up, looking decidedly uncomfortable. His companion glanced around, showing Julie a pretty face with eyes like violets set in a frame of deep auburn hair, all surrounded by the wide brim of her hat.

"Oh, Julie," Nick said. "This is Serena."

The young woman stood up, smiling with such friendliness that Julie was taken aback. A cool, slender hand grasped hers firmly.

"Julie. How lovely to meet you. Nick's told me so much about you."

"He has?" Startled, Julie glanced at Nick, who had his hands deep in his pockets and his eyes fixed on the grass beneath him.

"Yes, of course he has," Serena said merrily. "It's too bad of him to keep you out here broiling in this sun and watching boring old cricket. You'll want to freshen up after your journey. Did you bring a bag? Nick! Car keys, please." She held out a peremptory hand into which Nick obediently dropped his car keys, his glance sliding across Julie as one corner of his mouth twisted.

Serena slipped a hand beneath Julie's arm, turning her away. "You'll have to show me where he left the car. I'm so glad you could come to the party, Julie. Everyone's been longing to meet you."

"Thank you," was all Julie could think of to say. Things were going much too fast for her to make sense of them.

Briskly Serena removed Julie's overnight bag from the trunk of the MG and left the keys in its place. "If he'd had any sense, he'd have brought you up to the house first," she said, leading the way down the lane. Or are you a cricket fanatic?"

"I never watched it before," Julie admitted, beginning to realize that this slender woman with violet eyes and dark red hair actually lived in that lovely old house beyond the terraces. This was confirmed when Serena started to climb the first flight of steps between the stone urns.

"What do you think of the old homestead, then?" she asked.

"Oh—it's beautiful," Julie said, preoccupied by her own racing thoughts.

"Yes, I rather agree with you," Serena admitted. "We're lucky to have it. But today it's been sheer bedlam, what with caterers and one thing and another. Still, the ballroom's almost ready, and when I last looked they were finishing fixing the lights in the trees. Let's just hope they work."

They climbed three shallow flights of steps, with lawns and flower beds on either side, and came to the highest terrace, which was paved with old stone slabs and set with more tubs of flowers. Now the house reared over them, golden in the sunlight, its green drapes of rose leaves starred with blooms of pink and white, twined around the leaded windows and an iron-studded, round-topped door.

Serena opened the door and stepped into the broad hallway beyond. Rooms and passages led off the hallway, and in front of them a stairway of carved and shining wood led up to branch off and come at length to a gallery above. Paintings adorned the walls, and the polished parquet floor was protected by Turkish rugs in bright colors.

"Mother!" Serena called. "Mother, are you there?"

"In here, dear," came the faint reply.

Setting down Julie's bag, Serena beckoned her to follow, into a sitting room done in pink and gold, with brocade-covered furniture, paneled walls and ornate ceiling, a big marble fireplace, and two bay windows with a view of the valley. A woman stood by one of the tables, arranging roses in a silver bowl, but she turned and smiled pleasantly.

Despite pure white hair her face remained youthful, and a deceptively simple dress covered a slim figure. She wore a plain gold brooch at one shoulder.

"Mother, this is Julie Elliott," Serena announced. "Would you believe I found Nick watching the cricket, of all things?"

The woman dropped the rose she was holding and hurried forward, transferring her scissors to her left hand as she held out her right. "Julie, my dear!" she said warmly. "I'm so glad Nick persuaded you to come. Watching cricket, is he?" She laughed. "Yes, that sounds like Nick. He was a demon bowler when he was at school. Serena, why don't you show Julie up to her room? Make yourself entirely at home, my dear. We'll have tea shortly."

"You're very kind," Julie replied, feeling awkward because she had no idea how to address the woman since Nick had omitted to tell her the surname of these friends.

"Not at all, dear. We're delighted to have you here."

Returning to the hall, Serena carried Julie's bag up the stairs, taking the left-hand branch to the gallery and into a wide passageway with tables at intervals holding more bowls of flowers or pieces of porcelain.

"Here we are." Throwing open a door, Serena strolled into a room dominated by a four-poster bed. All the furniture was antique. The walls were covered in figured pink silk, matching the heavy drapes at the head of the bed.

"It's called the Rose Room, for obvious reasons,"

Serena said. "Just one thing—don't try drawing the bed curtains, or they might fall to pieces. They're nearly three hundred years old."

This piece of information was spoken with both pride and ruefulness, and Julie could hardly believe that she would be sleeping in that room, in that house where everything seemed touched by history.

"Does this house have a name?" she asked.

"Why, yes," Serena said in surprise. "Elmsford Hall. Didn't Nick tell you?"

"No, he didn't. He keeps doing things like this to me—surprising me. Have you, er, known him long?"

Violet eyes big as saucers stared at her, and Serena burst out laughing. "Only all my life!" But in face of Julie's bewilderment she sobered, a frown clouding her eyes. "What exactly *did* he tell you?"

"About you? Only that some friends of his were throwing a party and he wanted me to come. But, as I said, he likes surprising me. He thinks it's funny."

"Oh, really!" Serena frowned, seating herself in a brocade-covered chair that was probably Chippendale. "He did say he hadn't told you much, but honestly! It's a good job he isn't here, or he'd get a piece of my mind."

She seemed, Julie thought, to be on extremely intimate terms with Nick. "Your families are friends, are they?" she asked uncertainly.

"Julie . . ." Serena stood up, coming to touch Julie's arm as if to comfort her. "I can't understand why he hasn't told you, but to judge from what he was trying to say to me out there, I suppose he had his reasons. This place—Elmsford Hall—is his home. I'm his sister. And you've just met our mother."

Shock robbed Julie of words, but seeing her expression Serena exclaimed, "Oh, wait until I see that idiot brother of mine! What on earth does he think he's playing at? Listen, Julie . . . forget about him. You're welcome here. Very welcome. Mother took to you at once, I could see, and Dad will adore you—he likes beautiful blonds, in the nicest possible way. And there's Gran, mother's mother, who you'll meet later. She's a wee bit deaf and inclined to speak her mind, but you mustn't let her faze you. She likes people who stand up to her."

Recovering from her initial horror, Julie wondered what sins of discourtesy she had committed through ignorance. "I hope your mother didn't think I was rude. I didn't know what to call her."

"It's easy enough. She's Lady Ardon."

Julie swallowed hard to ease the lump in her throat, croaking, "*Lady* Ardon?"

"Oh, I'll kill Nick!" Serena said passionately. "Didn't he even tell you about that? Dad . . . well, Dad is a businessman, but he's also the Fourth Viscount Ardon of Elmsford. He inherited the title from his uncle, who died childless. We have this house, but most of the estate is in farms that are leased out—and of course there's the London flat."

"Where Nick lives?" Julie managed.

"Yes, that's right. Look—you get unpacked and settled in. Give yourself time to take it all in. I'll come back and fetch you when it's time for tea, so that you don't get lost. And remember—we're very glad to have you here. We were all thrilled when Nick said he was bringing you. When I tell them what he's done, throwing you in at the deep end like this—"

"No, don't," Julie begged. "Don't say anything. He meant it as a joke, I'm sure. He'll probably be sorry he wasn't here to see me react like Alice in Wonderland—that's what he called me once, and I do keep asking for it. I'm sorry, Serena, you must think I'm a fool."

"On the contrary, I like you a lot. It's that stupid brother of mine who's to blame. Anyway, I'll see you later. There's a bathroom just next door, if you need it."

"Serena . . ." Julie ventured as the other young woman made for the door. "If your father's a viscount, what does that make you and Nick?"

Serena made a face. "Officially, we're 'hons.' The Honorable Serena and the Honorable Nicholas—only he hasn't behaved very honorably toward you, has he? Just wait until I get my hands on him!"

Left alone in the quiet room, aware of the lovely old house around her, Julie paced the pink carpet thinking furiously, remembering clues that she had been too slow to pick up. So many little things clicked into place now. She stopped dead, staring out of the leaded window as she remembered coming out of the church at Sandringham and saying something about wishing to meet a real live lord. She recalled the strange little smile that had played across Nick's face as he replied that she would have to make do with him. Of course, he would inherit his father's title someday and become the Fifth Viscount Ardon of Elmsford! The realization turned her cold with shock. Why hadn't he told her? Oh, Serena was right; he had behaved abominably. Julie told herself she would never forgive him for this. Never!

When Serena returned, she led the way via another staircase into a maze of passages and alcoves, occasionally opening a door to show her visitor some of the rooms. "This is the billiard room. This leads into the long drawing room. And this is the ballroom. It used to be a mediaeval great hall. See, the musicians' gallery's still there, and that huge fireplace . . ."

People in overalls bustled about the room, putting finishing touches to decorations and lights or polishing the floor to a slippery sheen for dancing. Through three sets of wide French windows, Julie saw lawns beyond, edged by trees in which workmen on ladders struggled to fix strings of tiny lights, and in the valley a lake gleamed blue in the afternoon sun, a boathouse half hidden where woods came down to the water's edge.

"And we're having the buffet through here," Serena said, moving into an anteroom where more people were erecting tables, covering them with cloths of gleaming white linen. "This used to be the old kitchen and buttery, but it's all been altered over the years. Oh, dear, am I boring you?"

"Not at all," Julie assured her. "I only wish I could explore every inch."

They moved back along a corridor, into a newer part of the house, which was still two or three hundred years old, and through a sitting room where more

French doors stood open, leading into a wide-walled garden at the rear of the house. On the sunlit lawn a white table was set for tea, its matching chairs occupied by the members of Nick's family—including Nick himself. Julie dealt with the situation by virtually ignoring him as she was introduced to his grandmother, a formidable old woman wearing purple, and to his father. Viscount Ardon was the kind of man who grows more attractive with age, his hair winged with gray. Julie saw at once where Nick had got his good looks from. His father smiled at her and invited her to sit down, between himself and his son.

"So you're Nick's new girlfriend," the old lady barked, peering over the top of half-moon spectacles. "American, are you? Well, that's better than being French, I suppose. I never could stand the French."

"Mother!" Lady Ardon reprimanded, turning to Julie and smiling. "My mother pretends to dislike foreigners, but being half Rumanian herself she has no room to talk. Tea, my dear? With milk or lemon?"

"Lemon, please," Julie replied, wondering if she ought to correct the old lady's assumption that she was Nick's girlfriend. That was yet another bone she had to pick with the Hon. Nicholas, who lounged in the chair beside her, his eyes narrowed against the sun and no discernible expression on his face.

His family proceeded to make conversation, asking Julie about her family and her work, and how did she like England? Apart from odd, caustic remarks from the old lady, teatime passed very pleasantly, though all the time Julie seethed inside, wanting to do something violent to Nick every time he added a laconic comment. He knew very well that she was annoyed with him— she could tell by the sidelong glances he kept giving her as they ate thin cucumber sandwiches and tiny fancy cakes.

"Well, I mustn't sit here all day," Lady Ardon said eventually. "I must make sure the caterers are coping. Harry, will you just check that they've got those lights working at last? Oh, and Nick, it's time you were off to the station." Turning to Julie, she explained, "He has to meet my brother and his wife. At the moment the chauffeur's busy elsewhere. All the staff are up to their eyes getting ready for this evening. You won't mind if he deserts you for a while, I hope. Serena will entertain you, and you may like to have a rest before you start to get yourself ready. The party may go on until all hours."

As the tea party broke up, Julie had no chance to speak to Nick, who soon disappeared. It was Serena who took over, showing her around the grounds and more of the house before they both decided to go to their rooms and begin the preparation for the party.

"Is there some reason for the celebration?" Julie asked as they walked along the upper corridor.

"Yes," Serena replied. "I'll be twenty-one on Monday. But we thought it was better to have the ball today, so we can dance until dawn and sleep late tomorrow."

"I wish I'd known," Julie said. "I'd have brought you a present."

Smiling, Serena squeezed her arm. "It's enough that you're here. I think we're going to be really good friends, Julie. And—don't be too hard on Nick, will you? It was difficult for him. See you later."

She slipped away before Julie could ask what she meant.

Later, as she lay in the bath, Julie relived her meeting with Nick's family and was disturbed by the way they had all welcomed her so warmly, almost as if she really were Nick's ladyfriend. Hadn't he told them about Liz? Was he using Julie as a kind of smoke-screen?

Outside, long shadows crept across the valley before she finally looked at her reflection in the mirror. She had made up her face carefully and fastened her hair into a shining topknot, leaving a few curling ends to fall softly around her face and neck. The hairstyle emphasized the graceful line of her throat and shoulders, left bare but for spaghetti straps that supported the closely fitting bodice of her gown. From a ribbon belt, the skirt flared out in floaty layers that almost brushed the floor, echoing the colors of the sunset sky.

She had added a delicate but fashionably chunky necklace and bracelet of pure gold—a gift from her grandparents on her own twenty-first birthday more than a year before.

A light knock on the door announced the arrival of Serena, looking fragile in pale green. "Oh, you're ready!" she said, smiling. "You look marvelous, Julie. I'm just off to let mother know I'm around in case the guests start arriving, but there's no hurry. Nick said he'd be waiting in the library to bring you down when you're ready."

An unsteady pulse beat in Julie's throat as she made a final check of her appearance, gave an extra tweak to one of the wispy ringlets near her cheek, and decided that she was as ready as she would ever be. Taking a few deep breaths, which were supposed to calm her nerves, she picked up the gold-thread purse that matched her sandals and went into the corridor, making herself walk slowly as she tried to remember which was the library.

Of course—it was the last door on the left before the gallery. She stopped outside it, took another long, slow breath, and softly turned the handle.

The long room spread out before her, tall windows shedding fading daylight across polished mahogany tables. Three walls were lined with bookshelves crammed with priceless leather-bound volumes, while comfortable armchairs and settees waited to receive anyone who cared to sit down.

Nick stood by one of the tables, his head bent over an open book in his hand, unaware of her presence. For a moment Julie stood motionless, taking in the sight of him in a dinner jacket, gleaming white shirt, and black bow tie. How elegant he looked. How very different from the cameraman in jeans. But this is the Hon. Nicholas Tregarron, she thought, her heart twisting painfully.

Slowly she closed the door, making it click. Nick looked around questioningly, his glance taking in every inch of her as she moved toward him with her head held high, consciously graceful in the flowing skirt. She was gratified to see both surprise and admiration in his eyes.

"So you're female after all," he said drily.

"Did you doubt it?" Close to him, she noted how the stark black and white of his formal clothes brought out the red lights in his hair and emphasized his tan, making her feel stupidly weak and tremulous, though she struggled to regain some of her earlier annoyance with him.

Another leisurely glance ran over her, and when at last he looked into her face, no trace of mockery remained. "You look stunning."

"Thank you," she replied in a low voice. "I only wish that was literally true. You deserve to be stunned, Nick Tregarron. How could you bring me here without telling me—"

"I didn't know *how* to tell you," he broke in, laying the book on the table. "It's not something one announces at first meeting. At least, *I* don't. 'How do you do, I'm Lord Ardon's son'? It's not my style at all—especially not with someone I expect only to be working with. After that, you seemed so awed by titles and so forth I thought it best not to mention it, but the longer I delayed the harder it became to tell you, and then everything got so complicated. . . . Does it make a difference?"

"To what?"

"To us."

Julie caught her breath, wondering if she dare believe the grave inquiry in his eyes. "As working colleagues, you mean? No, what difference could it make? Though your family seems to be under the impression that there's something else between us."

"They jumped to conclusions," he said. "I rarely bring women home, and they're anxious to get me married off, that's all. Don't worry, I'll disabuse them when this evening is over. So I'm forgiven, am I?"

She searched his face, trying to find some clue to his thoughts, but the unreadable mask was firmly in place. She longed to put her arms around him to feel the shelter of his arms, and tell him that she loved him, but that was out of the question, especially now. He would think it was his title and his wealth that had influenced her.

"I guess so," she said.

"Good. Then shall we go down?"

He offered her his arm, and together they made their way down the stately stairs to join the guests who had begun to arrive. Julie put on a smile and an air of gaiety. Only she knew she was weeping inside, aching for this man she could never have.

She was introduced to so many people that she lost count. To judge by the butler's announcements as guests arrived, a good many of them were aristocrats: a couple of lords and their ladies, an extremely young and good-looking earl, who had his eye on Serena, a marquis, a scattering of younger-generation honorables. But most of them addressed each other by first names—even some silly nicknames—as drinks began to flow and the company moved into the ballroom. The men all wore formal evening dress while their wives and daughters drifted on a cloud of perfume, dressed in rainbow shades, a good many of the younger women having opted for the high-fashion white that was all the rage this season, with small touches of color in ribbons or sparkle in the weave of light materials.

The ballroom was lit by chandeliers, hung with sparkling streamers, and heady with the scent of flowers. In the centuries-old musicians' gallery, a six-piece band played lively tunes while the guests mingled below, talking and laughing over drinks, spreading across the shining floor and out through the open French windows onto lawns that sloped down to the lake, with colored lights now winking in the trees. Julie made small talk as efficiently as the rest, though she did wonder why no one was dancing. They seemed to be waiting for some signal.

She was chatting with a portly, gray-haired man known as Squiffy when a warm hand closed around her arm and Nick's voice murmured in her ear, "Do you fancy some fresh air?"

"Oh, come on, now," Squiffy objected. "You young-sters always claim the prettiest girls. She was talking to me! Oh, go on, then. But just watch yourself, Julie. If he tries to get you into the woods, yell for me and I'll come running."

Laughing, Julie allowed herself to be led away, out onto the lawn, where fairy lights twinkled behind moving leaves. More lights, she now saw, edged the narrow road that curved up to cross the lawn and disappear behind the rear of the house in the walled garage yard that Serena had shown her earlier.

"Enjoying yourself?" Nick said.

Renewing her party smile, she looked up at him. "I'm having a wonderful time. How about you?"

"Oh, wonderful." But he sighed as he said it, watch-ing her with sad brown eyes. "You're quite a success. Everyone's asking about you."

Concern wiped the smile from her face, not because of what he had said but because of the way he looked. "Nick . . ." she began but stopped as a sudden com-motion occurred in the ballroom. Nick's parents, accompanied by Serena, hurried out onto the lawn, their guests spilling after them. In the same moment, a flashing blue light drew Julie's attention to the car that was moving up from the main driveway, its headlights flickering behind the trees.

"What's happening?" she asked.

"It's a police car," Nick said.

"Police car?" she repeated incredulously. "Why, what's wrong?"

"Nothing's wrong. The guests of honor are arriving."

As the police car slid into sight, Julie saw another vehicle behind it—a black Rolls Royce that slid to a halt near where Lord and Lady Ardon stood waiting. The chauffeur climbed out, opened the door for his passengers, and saluted.

"I told you you wouldn't be sorry you came," Nick murmured as exclamations of pleasure broke from the assembled guests and Julie stared in disbelief at the attractive young couple now being greeted by Viscount Ardon and his wife and daughter.

It had been another day of surprises. But this outranked all the rest. The guests of honor were Charles, Prince of Wales, and his fiancée, the Lady Diana Spencer.

Nine

In a daze, Julie felt Nick's hand beneath her elbow gently propelling her toward the guests of honor. The prince wore a dinner jacket and bow tie, in common with all the other men present, while Lady Diana looked fresh and sweet in a full-skirted gown of white, sprigged with violets. To Julie's concern the bride-to-be looked a little pale as her blue eyes rested adoringly on her fiancé, who was laughing with Serena before he caught sight of Nick.

"Good to see you, Nick," His Royal Highness smiled. "How's the photography business going?"

"Pretty well, sir, thank you," Nick replied, shaking hands. "May I introduce Miss Julie Elliott, from Philadelphia?"

Later Julie would swear she stopped breathing when the prince gave her his hand, speaking to her charmingly and introducing her to Lady Diana, who smiled shyly. Then someone mentioned the fact of Julie's being a reporter, and the prince pretended horror. "I hope you haven't got a tape recorder hidden about you?"

"No, not tonight, sir," Julie said with amusement, then stepped aside as the prince moved on to greet other people while Lady Diana followed, chatting happily to Serena.

Centered around the illustrious newcomers, the assembly began to move slowly toward the ballroom, but Julie remained where she was, savoring the moment. She was aware of Nick still beside her, watching her.

"Well?" he prompted softly.

"Oh, Nick!" Impulsively, she turned to him, her eyes shining. "This is why you made me come, isn't it? You knew they would be here."

"I knew they'd been invited," he corrected. "There didn't seem any point in mentioning it in case they couldn't make it. But tonight is a private affair, Julie. I hope you understand that. They're both off their guard and trying to relax. You can write about the event, but don't quote them. Okay?"

"Yes, I understand."

"I hope you do. Apparently Lady Diana was upset earlier today. It's no wonder if she's feeling the strain. She's very young. An ordinary bride gets prewedding nerves. Think how much worse it must be for her, with the world watching."

Touched by his concern for the royal pair, she laid a hand on his arm. "It's all right, Nick, you don't have to explain. I'll respect their privacy, I swear."

"Thank you. But we'd best go inside. I shall probably be expected to dance with my mother."

Catching her hand, which seemed an entirely natural thing for him to do, he led her back toward the glitter of the ballroom.

The band began to play, and Julie was in time to see the Prince of Wales lead Serena onto the floor to begin the dancing. Nick's father claimed the hand of the laughing Lady Diana and, excusing himself, Nick approached his mother and swung her into the dance, which seemed to be the signal for every man to claim a partner. Julie found herself dancing with Squiffy, who took up their conversation where it had been interrupted earlier.

"Thought I'd better protect you from all the younger bucks," he puffed. "Nick certainly can't be jealous of me."

"Things aren't quite like that," Julie protested.

"No? Hah, don't give me that, my girl. I've got eyes." But he needed his breath for dancing, so the subject was dropped.

Time passed in a whirl of music. Partner after partner claimed Julie, even the handsome young earl, whose name was Adrian. Whether she danced or sat down to chat over drinks, Nick kept his distance. Even so, with her heightened awareness of him, she knew that he had his eyes on her as often as she sought him out among the crowd. She saw him dancing with Serena, with his aunt, even with his grandmother, and then she watched as he escorted Lady Diana onto the floor.

Suddenly she became aware that Prince Charles was nearby, chatting easily with the people around him. He caught her eye and gestured to where his fiancée was waltzing with Nick. "Shall we do the same, Miss Elliott?"

Fortunately her feet were in control of themselves, even though her tongue had tied itself in knots, but the prince talked so naturally as they danced that soon she forgot her nerves and found herself joking with him. Somewhere close by a flashbulb made brief lightning, but Julie was too immersed in her conversation with the prince to take any more notice than he did.

"I expect you'll be glad when Wednesday is over, sir," she remarked.

"Yes, these big occasions can be nervewracking—not so much for me, since I'm used to it, but Diana's under a great deal of pressure." Then grinning, he added, "But my main worry is that my brother Andrew might forget the ring."

Julie laughed with him. Then the music ended and he escorted her to where Lord Ardon stood with Lady Diana. Julie found herself included in their group, feeling almost as relaxed as they so obviously were.

All too soon, the royal couple took their leave and returned to their limousine. As Julie joined the exodus to wish them farewell, she knew she had experienced an honor for which every other reporter would have given his eye teeth. Let the rest fight to get pictures of the prince playing polo tomorrow; Julie had danced with him. She had an exclusive story to write, though the trust with which she had been received made her resolve that she would be careful how much she revealed.

As the cars moved away she mused that the prince was just as attractive, charming, and amusing as she had always thought. Now, however, he was only the second most attractive man in the world. She was reminded that her own story would be denied its fairy-tale ending.

Determined not to give way to sadness, she accepted at once when another young man joined her and asked for a dance, but as they walked back to the ballroom, Nick's tall figure appeared in the doorway, barring their entry.

"I've just asked her to dance," her prospective partner said. "You don't mind, do you, old man?"

"As a matter of fact, *old man*," Nick replied heavily, "I do mind. I haven't danced with the girl all evening, and she's supposed to be with *me*. Get lost, Gerry."

Gerry bristled but decided against making an argument of it, though before he moved away he remarked to Julie, "I'll be around, if you find you prefer to dance with a gentleman."

Folding his arms, Nick leaned in the doorway, peering narrowly after the departing Gerry. "Thought you could go on avoiding me all night, did you?" he demanded.

"Have you been drinking?" she asked.

"Of course I have. Haven't you? But I'm not drunk, if that's what you mean, though, with the mood I'm in, I may well go on a bender before the night's out. It's a fine thing when I bring a girl home to meet my family, introduce her to the Prince of Wales, and then I can't get near her for panting hordes of men who are supposed to be my friends—or my father's friends, to add insult to injury."

"You haven't seemed to be trying very hard," Julie observed, gently reproving, though he didn't sound entirely serious. "I danced with Prince Charles, too. Did you see?"

"Everybody here saw it! *And* you were getting on extremely well with Adrian, who is supposed to be Serena's escort. I know he's an earl and a multi-millionaire, but—"

She peered up at him, though with the ballroom lights behind him it was impossible to see his face clearly. "If I didn't know better," she broke into his tirade, "I might think you were displaying all the symptoms of the possessive male."

"You amaze me," he said dryly, reaching for her hand to draw her into the ballroom.

But as she stepped through the door, the music stopped. A voice announced that the buffet was about to be served. And a few moments later a disco beat started up from a hidden sound system, filling the room with the sound of drums and guitars.

"Oh, hell!" Nick groaned as his sister and most of the younger generation rushed eagerly onto the floor. "I'd forgotten she'd asked to have jungle music in the interval. I'm not in the mood for that at the moment. How about some supper? Tell you what—you find us a seat outside, and I'll bring the food."

On the lawn, small groups of people stood enjoying the warm night air away from the insistent beat in the ballroom. Some of the guests relaxed on seats ranged around the area, while others sprawled on the grass taking their supper al fresco. Julie made her way to where a vacant bench stood a little distance away beneath the spreading branches of a beech tree. The evening had become unreal, like some crazy dream, but she was content to let it continue to flow over her.

"Here, Nick," she called when she saw him appear, a laden plate in one hand and two glasses in the other.

"I hope you don't mind sharing a plate," he said. "I couldn't manage two."

146

They picnicked there beneath the tree, with twinkling lights above and music spilling from the ballroom twenty yards away. Julie felt totally happy, letting herself drift on the magic of the night. Let tomorrow bring what it would, tonight she had Nick beside her and wonderful memories to dream about.

"We ought to go back inside," he said eventually, breaking an amicable silence as he turned moon-dark eyes to her face.

"I suppose so."

He stood up, offering her his hand, and as she came to her feet, he slipped his free arm around her, bending to kiss her full on the lips, causing that cataclysmic upheaval inside her. When he lifted his head she struggled to get her breath, her brain spinning.

"I've been wanting to do that all night," he said softly. "You've had me so confused I haven't known how to behave. But here, now, with a few drinks inside me. . . . Allow me this, will you? Just for tonight?"

She had no idea what he meant, but before her lips could frame a question, his mouth captured hers again, and she no longer cared about explanations. All that mattered was his warm strength in the friendly shadows of the tree, as she gave full rein to the feelings that engulfed her.

How long they remained there she never knew, except that it wasn't long enough. Forever wouldn't have been long enough, not with her love for him growing with every passing second, bursting into a fire that caught both of them up in its passion. But eventually they drew apart, looking at each other wonderingly in the shadows of the tree.

Burning dark eyes, their depths filled with tenderness, considered every feature of her face. "You look as if you've been kissed," he murmured.

"I wonder why," she replied on an unsteady laugh. "I'd better tidy myself up before I go back. Is there a side door?"

"Yes, I'll show you the way. But don't be long, will you? I want to dance with you. Preferably a very slow waltz."

147

* * *

The first streaks of dawn were graying the sky before she at last crawled into bed, very tired but crazily happy in the memory of those last few hours, dancing only with Nick as the lights in the ballroom dimmed. As the ball ended, he had escorted her to her room, kissed her with slow tenderness, and finally, reluctantly, left her to her dreams.

Strangely enough, those dreams were muddled and frightening, consisting of scenes in which she was forcibly parted from Nick or rushed screaming in search of him only to fling open a door and see Liz Bentham laughing at her.

By the time she woke it was past noon, with less than four days left before she must go home to the States.

Now she had time and solitude enough to ponder over the previous evening, and those ponderings brought her little comfort. She must have been out of her mind, high on excitement and champagne. *Just for tonight*, Nick had said, and she had let him hold her, kiss her, caress her . . . because she was such a fool that she had wished to snatch every drop of joy from the moment. But now, in the cool daylight, she felt as though she had been used, just to pass a few hours for him before he returned to London and Liz Bentham. Julie felt almost sick remembering how she had responded so willingly.

That she meant very little to him had been proved by their talk in the library earlier: *My family jumped to conclusions. I'll disabuse them when this evening is over.* She could well imagine the conversation that might take place as he explained that she had been just a passing fancy, just a wide-eyed American girl bowled over by the things he had shown her.

As she bathed and dressed, such thoughts intensified into bitterness, until she felt she had grown an armor that not even Nick Tregarron could scratch. Not until much later did she wonder if her subconscious had been trying to harden her against Nick in order to ease their inevitable parting.

148

She was glad now that she had brought along another outfit for this Sunday, one of her favorites—a skirt and top in clinging jersey silk of a creamy-blond color that almost matched her hair. In it, she felt very much a member of the influential Elliotts of Philadelphia, determined to prove that she was no insignificant little backwoods hick to be made use of and tossed aside.

Reaching the gallery, she heard the soft bronze strokes of a gong sounding along the passageways below, and she saw Nick, rising from a chair in the hall, becoming still as he caught sight of her. Her own emotions were in uproar as she surveyed his lean figure strikingly dressed in black shirt and cords, but she composed her face and went slowly down the stairs, well aware of how she looked—slim and golden, the sleek skirt flirting round her knees to draw attention to her legs and slender ankles, set off by spike-heeled sandals. And from the look on Nick's face, she had created the desired effect.

He moved toward her, lifting a hand as if to touch her, his eyes asking questions about her aloofness.

"Was that the lunch gong?" she asked coolly.

The hand dropped as if she had bitten it, and his eyes narrowed. "Yes, sort of. We usually have aperitifs in the green drawing room first."

"I hope I'm not the last down."

"No, several people haven't surfaced yet. I've only been up for half an hour myself. That was quite a party."

"Wasn't it, though?" She turned away, knowing her attitude puzzled him. "Which is the green drawing room?"

"Are you angry with me?" he asked, low-voiced. "Last night . . ."

"I really don't remember much about last night," she lied. "Not after the Prince and Lady Diana left. I must have had too much champagne. I can't drink—as you know very well."

A glance at him told her the barb had gone home—deeper than she intended, perhaps, but she steeled herself against feeling sorry for him. If he believed that alcohol had made her respond to him—at the ball and in his studio the night before—then so much the better.

Voices from above warned her that other people were coming from their rooms in response to the gong's summons. His aunt and uncle appeared, and both Julie and Nick were obliged to reply to their greetings and join them as they went to take aperitifs with the remaining guests.

Julie chose to sit by Squiffy, who was flattered by her company and kept her engaged during drinks and then all through lunch. Fifteen people sat down to eat in the paneled dining room, and if any of them wondered why she deliberately stayed away from Nick, Julie didn't care. Let him explain that, too, when he explained the rest.

"Robin and I thought we'd go riding this afternoon," Serena announced as the gathering lingered over coffee. "Anyone want to come? Julie, do you ride? I'd love to show you the valley. You can borrow a pair of my jodhpurs, I'm sure they'll fit. Or are you in a hurry to get back to London?"

She looked for answer to Nick, who shrugged and said, "I'm not. It's up to Julie."

"Sounds like a fine idea," Julie agreed, smiling at Serena.

"Oh, wonderful! Excuse us, everyone, please. Come on, Julie, let's get you kitted out."

By the time the two young women had changed into shirts and jodhpurs, Serena's cousin Robin had gone ahead to the stables to have horses saddled. Serena got out her sports car and took Julie down to the stables, which were housed in the gatehouse with its central archway and clock tower. To Julie's chagrin, Nick had accompanied Robin and was apparently intending to come riding, too. His look said that if she had thought to escape him, she had better think again.

They rode along the valley, the women just ahead of the men, along a bridle path through the woods beside the lake, where the sun dappled down among summer leaves. After a while they came to more open downland that undulated into the distance.

"Who's for a race?" Serena cried. "Up to the old windmill. Come on, Robin. Fifty pence on it."

She nudged her heels into the horse, urging it into a gallop, with Robin thudding in hot pursuit. As they moved away, Nick edged his mount alongside Julie's.

"We must talk," he said somberly.

"Yes, I had a feeling you'd arranged all that," she replied, nodding after the retreating pair. "It's all so easy for you, isn't it?"

"In what way?"

"In every way. I've been going over everything that's happened since I arrived in London, and it seems you've misled me all along the line. For a start you kept pretending to hate the very idea of the royal wedding, but actually you know Prince Charles. You know him personally."

"I was at school with him, at Gordonstoun," he told her, his eyes on his horse's neck as he stroked it. "And we met again in the navy—I was a naval officer for five years. And before that—" As he paused, he sighed heavily. "We lived near Sandringham. Serena used to play with Lady Diana and her sisters. Our families knew each other pretty well, and—and there were times when we mixed socially with the royal family."

It was worse than she had thought. A pall of depression settled over her as she realized the extent to which she had been fooled. "I suppose that's why it was so easy for you to arrange that meeting with Earl and Countess Spencer—and with that naval cook at Chatham." As another puzzle was solved, she turned to him in anguish. "Those photographs! Of Lady Diana in that treehouse—"

"I sent them," he admitted. "I took them myself, when I first began fooling about with cameras. The other girl with her was Serena. But you were pleased with them, weren't you? You said they were a real scoop."

"So they were! You could have sold them for a fortune."

A spasm of anger crossed his face as he looked across at her. "I had no intention of selling them! I wanted to give them to you."

"Why?"

"Because you were so anxious to make a success of this job!" he said savagely. "That was my function, wasn't it—to be of use to you? You were floundering. You hadn't the first idea where to start. Now Jim Dawes thinks you're a brilliant newspaperwoman, and when you get home your editor will probably promote you. Isn't that what you want?"

"Not this way! I wanted to do it myself, not have someone pulling strings for me. Don't you understand that?"

"All I understand is that I was doing my best to please you, but I appear to have gone about it the wrong way, as usual."

"It would be different if you had *told* me!" she exclaimed. "But to let me believe it all happened by chance. . . . It's not that I'm ungrateful, Nick. I just wish I'd known you were using your influence on my behalf. I suppose you had a word with the Emanuels, too—made them change their minds about seeing me?"

His lip curled derisively. "No, that's one thing I didn't do. Nor did I write any of your articles for you. All I did was provide you with the raw material. And now you've got another exclusive—how you danced with the Prince of Wales at a private ball no other journalist knew about. I've even got a picture of it, in case you're interested. But you'd better make the most of it because that's all I intend to do. If you want a firsthand account of the wedding ceremony, you'll have to interview someone else."

Disturbed by his intense bitterness, she took a moment to realize what he meant. "You're going to the wedding?"

"My family and I have been invited to attend the ceremony at Saint Paul's, yes. I was saving that to surprise you with, but apparently you don't like surprises. Shall we go back now? There doesn't seem to be any point in prolonging this conversation, and I'm sure you're anxious to get back to London—to write about last night and make your readers drool over the romance of it all."

He jerked his horse around, and after a moment Julie followed, miserably aware that she had handled that scene all wrong. She had been spoiling for a fight, but now that it had happened it brought no satisfaction; she felt small and mean, ashamed of herself and horribly certain that she had ruined the tiny chance she might have had with Nick.

They drove back to London in icy silence. Remembering how his parents had said goodbye and told her how much they hoped to see her again, Julie could only pray that she hadn't offended the Ardons. They had known that something was amiss, though they were too well-bred to say anything about it.

In the city the traffic crawled at a slow pace that had Nick swearing under his breath. Every street seemed crammed with vehicles and people. When eventually they arrived at the penthouse apartment, Nick threw his suitcase into his room and tossed Julie a key.

"Lock up when you go, and if I'm not back when you've finished work, don't wait up for me. See you."

The door slammed behind him, and Julie looked at the key in her hand, her eyes stinging. Most probably he was going to prowl the crowded streets with his camera, but feminine instinct reminded her that it was Sunday. Liz Bentham had no show to perform on Sundays. Oh, damn! She didn't have time to cry. There was work to be done—another exclusive article to impress Hank Freeman.

At the IP office she discovered that she had missed the big event of that day—a dress rehearsal for the wedding processions, complete with coaches, horses, mounted escorts, and bands. Tens of thousands of people had watched the spectacle, apparently, which explained the crowds that still filled the streets. Julie thought glumly that that just proved what kind of newshound she was—while all the excitement was taking place, she had been asleep.

It was after nine when she returned to the flat. She unlocked the door hoping to see a light on, but the place was silent and dark. Nick had not returned. Probably he would be gone all night.

Having fixed herself some supper, she sat down to watch television and saw film of another event she had missed. In Oxford Street, a mile-long table had been set up for a party for hundreds of underprivileged and disabled children, who had eaten hamburgers and ice cream and toasted the royal bride and groom in Coca-Cola. That would have made a good human-interest piece, if only she had been there.

Depressed and tired after the traumatic two days she had just lived through, she went to bed and eventually slept, her arms wrapped tightly round a pillow that was damp from tears.

In the morning the flat was quiet, nothing changed from the previous night. As she made herself a light breakfast, she wondered if Nick had stayed with Liz Bentham all night or whether he had gone out already, to avoid seeing her. Then to her intense relief she heard him in the bathroom and the inner hall, and eventually he appeared, garbed in his familiar jeans with a blue shirt, though he looked as if he had not slept.

"I made you some coffee," Julie said, handing him a cup. "Aren't you well? You look terrible."

"So would you, if you hadn't slept for two nights," he replied, and slumped at the bar with his head in his hands.

Watching him uncertainly, she had to steel herself against an urge to put her arms around him. "Did you get in very late last night?"

"What difference does it make?" he snapped. "Leave me alone, will you?"

She poured herself another cup of coffee and retreated to the sitting room, to a big comfortable chair by the window, where she could see down across

154

Kensington Gardens as the city came to bustling life.

"What have you got planned for today?" Nick asked after a while.

"I won't know until I've called the office to see what's going on."

"But you'll want me with you?"

"If you don't mind."

"I took this damned assignment," he said roughly. "I'll see it through to the bitter end."

There were all manner of replies she could have made to that, but she felt too low in spirits to indulge him when he was obviously in a quarrelsome mood.

It was a hectic day, beginning with a press conference at which journalists of all nationalities were briefed by a secretary from Buckingham Palace, who deftly avoided giving away any secrets, as usual. Among the throng Julie glimpsed Barbara Walters, whose obvious expertise made Julie despair.

The *Today* team, headed by Tom Brocaw and Jane Pauley, were transmitting their program live from The Mall, their desk under the trees against a backdrop of the palace, surrounded with all the hardware that was necessary—huge vans, cameras, miles of cable. Everywhere, TV crews and cameramen jostled to get the best shots, many of them taking pictures of others taking pictures, since the vast media coverage was in itself news.

Wedding fever filled the city with heady joy. Along the wedding route spectators were camped out to stake their places, some of them being interviewed by roving reporters while smiling policemen looked on. In the welcome sunshine everyone smiled and laughed, their cares forgotten, if only for a few days.

Eventually, Julie and Nick returned to Saint Paul's, where policemen and women in blue coveralls scanned the grounds with metal detectors as part of the security operation. The cathedral itself had been closed to the general public to enable final preparations to get into top gear. Masses of flowers were being installed, and below the steps a thick layer of sand had been laid to prevent the carriage horses from slipping. Curious crowds watched as officials checked and rechecked everything, from the drape of flags to the position of TV cameras.

In the midst of all this, Mrs. Nancy Reagan, wife of the president of the United States, arrived to lay a wreath at the American Memorial Chapel, and soon after her departure Julie saw another car draw up, bringing Prince Charles to a last rehearsal of the ceremony. He climbed the steps, waving to the happy crowd. Then as he reached the colonnade he tripped, saved himself and turned to grin, sharing the crowd's amusement—though Julie had sensed the momentary horror that had held everyone breathless. She was amused to see that officials with the prince paused to frown at the offending step that had almost caused the downfall of the heir to the throne.

Finally, with her notebook overflowing, she returned to the IP office trying to concentrate on the article she would write, though her thoughts kept veering to remind her that another hectic day lay ahead, then the wedding itself, and after that. . . .

"Phew!" Maddie Venables greeted. "All happening, isn't it? How are you doing, Julie? I haven't seen you for days. Did you find somewhere to stay?"

"Oh—yes, thank you." Too fraught to face the explanations that must ensue if she said exactly *where* she was staying, Julie made for the stairs. "Excuse me, Maddie. I don't want to lose my train of thought."

Her article concerned the heightened excitement she had sensed in London, with quotes from many of the people she had spoken to that day. As she typed the final draft, a photograph was tossed on the desk beside her and Jim Dawes's voice said simply, "How?"

The shot was a black and white photograph showing her held lightly in Prince Charles's arms against a background of other dancers in the ballroom at Elmsford Hall. "You read my story, didn't you?"

"Of course I did. Then I had it wired, along with this

picture. Hank's just been on the phone, asking the same things I want to know. How did you manage it? When did you meet Viscount Ardon and get invited to this ball? Family connections?"

Pushing back her hair, Julie looked up at him. "Nick Tregarron is Lord Ardon's son. Didn't you know?"

"Well, I'll be—!" the bureau chief exclaimed. "He's kept that pretty quiet. They'll want to interview him, too, then."

"Interview?" she asked.

"NBC got on to me when this hit the wires. Lord, Julie, don't you realize what a scoop this was? Not even Barbara Walters could manage it. She was told that it took six months to organize a talk with Prince Charles. She got herself invited to a garden party at the palace, and she just managed to get a few words with him. *You* danced with him! But you've played it all down. You didn't write what he said or what Lady Diana said. *That's* what they want to know. NBC want you to go along to the Intercontinental Hotel, where they're all staying. You're to see a man called—"

"I can't do that," Julie said.

He stopped, his mouth open, even his hair looking surprised as it stood in spikes around his head. "Why not?"

"Because it was a private party. I'd be breaking a confidence."

To her relief, the door at the far end of the room came open, and Nick strode in to make his way around the desks. Jim Dawes began trying to persuade him to be interviewed about his friendship with the prince, but Nick said firmly that to disclose what members of the royal family had said in private was just not done.

"So you've joined the club," Nick said as he drove her back through the city.

"Club?"

"Those of us who just don't tell what we know about certain things. I seem to remember you complaining about that. There's nothing to stop you from going on TV and talking about the ball, though. Think how proud your parents would be."

Julie had already thought about that. Yes, her parents would have been thrilled to see her on the *Today* show. It could have meant another step up for Julie Joanna Elliott, newsperson. But somehow the idea didn't appeal to her. "I'd have let you down," she said. "I'm not as good at being evasive as some people are. I'd be tempted to boast and end up telling everything. It's safer not to risk it."

He sent her one of his enigmatic looks. "Then thank goodness no one knows where you're staying. I appreciate your discretion, Julie, but if you're ambitious you have to make full use of lucky breaks."

"You sound like my grandfather," she replied, no longer sure that she had that much ambition. She had been thrilled to meet the prince, of course, but she felt no great sense of professional triumph.

As they arrived at the flat, Nick nodded toward one of the glass tables. "Something came for you."

The something was a large white envelope. Frowning, Julie opened it and took out the card inside, which was headed by a gold crest. *The Lord Chamberlain*, she read, *is Commanded by The Queen and The Duke of Edinburgh to invite Miss Julie Elliott. . . .* She had to read it three times before her eyes believed what her brain was telling her.

"I told the prince about your wildest dream," Nick said quietly. "I knew there'd be a spare seat because my father's been summoned to an important business meeting in Zurich. I didn't say anything because I wasn't sure anything would come of it. Just don't be mad at me for it."

"Mad at you?" she breathed, lifting tear-filled eyes, so full of excitement that nothing else mattered. "Oh, Nick!" Unable to stop herself, she threw her arms round his neck and kissed his cheek, one hand still clutching the wedding invitation that had her name written on it.

When she tried to draw away, his arms looped around her waist to prevent her, and he looked down at her sadly. "All I ever wanted was to please you," he said. "I didn't mean to take over, or undermine your confidence. If I'd known it would annoy you, I'd have told you the truth sooner, but I suppose part of me was enjoying teasing you. I thought you understood that."

"I did." Troubled, she searched his face, trying to etch it into her memory for all the years ahead when she would be without him. "That wasn't the real reason I was upset."

"Then what was it?"

"It doesn't matter." Pressing her face to the warmth of his throat, she fastened her arms tightly about him, pushing thoughts of Liz Bentham to the back of her mind. What was happening between her and Nick was a kind of madness, a temporary aberration that would fade once they parted, she to return to the States and he to resume his normal life. But here and now they were together, and she needed his closeness.

For a few silent moments they stood holding each other, then Nick laid his hands on her waist and eased her away, dark eyes fixed on her face.

"We shouldn't," he said simply. "Go and sit down and I'll fix you a drink. We've got something to celebrate: we shall both be going to the wedding."

Ten

That Tuesday passed in a whirl for Julie. She spent most of the day, or so it seemed, in fitting rooms trying on outfit after outfit to find something suitable to wear to the royal wedding, and eventually, when she had almost given up hope, she returned to the Emanuel salon in Brook Street and there found a sleeveless dress and matching jacket in striped pink silk. It was terribly expensive, but well worth it, she felt. Lady Diana had brought romance back to fashion, and pale pinks seemed just right for Julie. She also found a hat to match, with a white flower tucked under the wide, flattering brim.

Everywhere along the route now, people had settled down to wait, bringing their sleeping bags, camping stoves, and bulging bags of food and drink. Most of them wore some item of wedding significance, fancy hats decked with the Union Jack or ribbons in red, white and blue, and many of them had small flags ready to wave if a TV camera passed by or one of the patient London policemen came up to do yet another security check. Even though some of the people had already been in place for twenty-four hours, their spirits remained high, infecting the city with gaiety.

"Been shopping?" Maddie Venables inquired when

Julie looked into the office to check that nothing earthshaking had occurred while she had been otherwise occupied.

"I've just been blowing all my savings," she admitted happily. "I'm going to the wedding, Maddie."

"You're what?" Maddie gasped.

The tale took some time to recount, but on that day Julie was past caring. She didn't even feel very guilty about playing hooky from work because tomorrow she was going to have the story of a lifetime: how it had been to be physically present in Saint Paul's when the Prince of Wales married his fairy-tale lady.

Leaving Maddie nearly green with envy, Julie checked with Jim Dawes that all was going well and, satisfied to at least have shown her face, she made her way back to Kensington with her purchases.

As she pushed her way into Nick's apartment, laden with boxes and bags, a female voice called from the inner hallway, "Is that you, Nick?"

Julie froze, her blood running cold in the moment before Serena appeared across the sitting room.

"Oh, Julie, hello. Do you know where Nick is?"

Expelling her relief in a great sigh, Julie dumped her shopping bags and boxes on the nearest chair. "I haven't seen him since this morning. He went out to take some more of his offbeat pictures, as he calls them. You gave me a shock. For a moment I thought you were someone else."

"You look worn out," Serena said with sympathy. "Shall I make some tea? By the way, I gather your invitation came. I'm so glad."

As Serena put the kettle on the stove, Julie trailed across the room to flop down on one of the stools by the bar. "Did Nick know you were coming?"

"Yes, of course," Serena said in surprise. "Is that another thing he omitted to tell you? I'm staying over tonight and tomorrow, because of the wedding. Mother's in town, too, staying with friends. The car will pick her up tomorrow and then call here for us. Isn't it exciting? I can't wait. But I wonder how Diana's feeling. In her shoes, I'd be a nervous wreck. Let's take this tea into the bedroom, and I'll show you my outfit."

The twin-bedded room looked like disaster in a fashion store; apparently Serena had been unpacking when Julie arrived, and her clothes were flung across both beds. They spent a pleasant few minutes admiring each other's choice of apparel for the wedding, then Serena began to tidy up, stowing things away in the wardrobe and drawers.

"So this is where I left this slip!" she exclaimed, lifting out a filmy concoction of silk and lace. "I've been looking for it everywhere. Honestly, I have a head like a sieve."

Julie stared at the garment as it was laid away in the drawer with the other feminine items that had caused her so much heartache. "It's yours?" she managed in a strangled voice. "And the coat and the shoes?"

Closing the drawer, Serena turned, looking bewildered. "Yes, of course. I often stay here when I'm in town. Why, what did you think?"

"I thought . . ." Her throat wouldn't seem to work properly. "No, nothing. It doesn't matter. Serena, were you here—when would it be?—two Fridays ago? I phoned Nick and—"

"And I answered," Serena said. "I remember telling him you sounded nice, and he played it all down—you know how men are. But I suspected there was more to it, even then." Round-eyed and teasing, she laughed. "Don't tell me you thought he had some secret lover? Julie Elliott, I'm surprised at you. But I'm afraid I must get on. I have a date tonight. Adrian's taking me to a party at the Sheraton Hotel. We'll be watching the royal fireworks from there."

Listening to the bathwater thunder into the tub, Julie told herself she ought to be elated. She had misinterpreted two of the clues concerning Nick's relationship with Liz Bentham. But she could not persuade herself that she had made a mistake that day when she saw them together, and when she had asked him about the actress, he had not denied knowing her.

The phone in the living room began to ring, and Julie left the bedroom to answer it.

"If that's Adrian," Serena called, "tell him I'll be ready at seven-thirty, as arranged."

The caller was not Adrian; it was Nick, who said that he would not be home until late. He had to meet someone to discuss his next commission, and then he intended to go to Hyde Park to take pictures of the fireworks display.

"Why don't you and Serena go along there?" he added. "She has arrived, I take it?"

"Yes, she's in the bath. Got a heavy date tonight, apparently. But don't worry about me. I'll be fine."

Sighing heavily, she sank into a chair. She had half planned to make a meal for him, a cozy supper for two on their last evening together. Tomorrow would be frantic, with the wedding taking up most of the day, followed by a session at International Press, and then she had to pack, and Serena would be there. At this rate she might never be alone with Nick again. But perhaps that was just as well.

She turned on the television just in time to watch the official interview with tomorrow's bride and groom, who had been filmed while sitting in the summerhouse in the palace grounds. Serena rushed in and out, wrapped in towels and in various stages of undress, trying to watch the program, too, before she finished dressing. When Adrian arrived to collect her, they generously offered to take Julie along with them to the party, but she declined. The role of fifth wheel had never been one she enjoyed.

So she spent the evening alone, watching the spectacular fireworks on TV and drinking coffee. The entire royal family were in Hyde Park that night, with all their VIP guests and thousands of humbler persons, all gathered to witness Prince Charles's lighting of the first of a chain of beacons, which were to spread the length and breadth of the land in celebration. Lady Diana did not attend the occasion. During the interview she had said that she would be "tucked up in bed early" this last night of her life as a single girl.

Watching the prince perform the informal ceremony with his usual aplomb and humor, Julie found it incredible to think that she had met and danced with him. Already the episode had taken on the shape of an impossible dream. Maybe in six months' time the memory of Nick, too, would be unbelievable. Maybe then it would stop hurting.

Perhaps if he came home and they could talk. . . . But the evening wore on. The television relayed the excitement of fireworks, cannons, bands, and choirs, and from the window Julie could see the glare, the rockets and dazzling showers of colored sparks. But the show went on until late, and knowing she had a full day ahead, Julie went to bed. What was the point of waiting up for Nick when it would only mean more emotional torture?

By the time she rose very early on the morning of July 29, Nick had already gone out with his camera to snatch a few pictures of the early preparations and the crowds that now lined the route in a solid mass of humanity. Julie and Serena saw the growing expectation on TV, which had interviewers out among the excited spectators, as well as experts in the studio to discuss aspects of the wedding, including much speculation about the wedding dress. Julie heard fleeting snatches of the programs as she and Serena bathed and dressed, with Serena constantly watching the clock and chafing that if Nick was late they would have to leave without him. They had to be in their seats at Saint Paul's before ten o'clock.

They were almost ready before they heard Nick come in and start running the shower. While he dressed, the two young women waited in the living room, Julie in her pink silk dress and jacket and wide-brimmed hat, and Serena in lilac and white, her pillbox hat trimmed with ostrich feathers.

"It's about time!" Serena exclaimed when at last her brother made his appearance.

In morning dress, his athletic figure looked devastating, making Julie feel a little shy of him. The Honorable Nicholas Tregarron, she repeated to herself, feeling that he had moved away from her yet again. But when he smiled at her, her heart jolted in answer.

"You both look marvelous," he said. "We've still got fifteen minutes before the car arrives. I'd like to take a picture of us all, for the record. I've got the studio set up."

Despite Serena's protests that there wasn't time for pictures, they went up to the studio, and he had them pose for him, putting the camera on a delayed setting, which gave him time to rush and stand between them so that all three of them were in the shot.

"That's quite enough of that," Serena said when the camera clicked. "I'm going down. If the car arrives and they phone up for us, we shan't hear it."

"Stop panicking!" Nick ordered, but she had gone. Shaking his head, he glanced at Julie. "I'd like to take one of you, on your own. Stay where you are. Chin up a little. Smile . . . thank you."

"You're not taking your camera to Saint Paul's, are you?" she asked, stepping down from the dais.

"I'd like to, but it might not be appreciated," he replied. "I've got someone else taking actual wedding shots for me. Not that I intend to use many of them myself. There'll be quite enough gooey snaps floating around when this day is over."

"Oh, of course—you're not interested in the romantic side, are you?" she said. "I'd quite forgotten. How on earth did you bring yourself to accept the invitation and get dressed up that way?"

He gave her a lopsided grin. "Like a tailor's dummy? It wasn't easy. I'd prefer to be among the crowd in my old jeans, except"—the amusement faded from his eyes as he laid his hands warmly on her shoulders, lowering his voice to a deep, intimate note—"that I'd rather be with you today. You'll be the most beautiful woman in Saint Paul's."

"It's here!" Serena's shrill call rang up the stairs. "The car's here. Oh, come on, you two!"

"Have dinner with me tonight," Nick murmured. "I've booked a table for nine o'clock. Can you be finished work by then?"

Wishing her heart would behave itself, she nodded, too overcome to risk speaking.

In the courtyard outside the apartment block waited a sleek and gleaming Rolls Royce, with a uniformed chauffeur. An official number was taped to the windshield. Lady Ardon already occupied the backseat, dressed in blue with a feathered turban.

Along the Strand, a long line of limousines moved slowly between sidewalks crammed with people. More revelers were grouped on balconies and rooftops and in windows, a colorful sea of smiling faces and waving flags, all there to wish the bridal couple well.

One by one the cars ahead paused to allow their passengers to alight, and eventually it was Julie's turn to step out, among a throng of pastel fashions, morning suits, and dress uniforms at whom the curious crowds stared, trying to identify familiar faces. She had never experienced such an atmosphere of expectant joy, and she was proud to have been granted a small part in it.

Some of the guests lingered on the steps outside the side door of the cathedral, others made their way inside. Uniformed ushers checked everyone's invitation, and for a second Julie was afraid she might lose that treasured memento. But the soldier returned the card to her and, carefully putting it into her pink purse, she walked beside Serena, following Nick and his mother into a brilliantly lit and flower-decked Saint Paul's.

Organ music swelled and diminished like the sea, softly flowing over the hum of voices as guests were conducted to their seats. To her delight, Julie found herself quite near the front, between Nick and Serena, where she would have a good view of everything that occurred, and she felt a momentary sense of glee as she realized that she would be closer than any other media person, since most of them were now locked in their unobtrusive boxes and had been sweating there since nine o'clock, some for longer.

Places slowly filled, a sea of hats, uniforms, and male heads. Choristers moved in a procession to the choir stalls; the plastic cover over the red carpet was discreetly removed. While Nick gave her a low-voiced commentary, explaining and identifying, presidents, prime ministers, and crown princes took their seats. Shortly afterward a group of gentlemen-at-arms in plumed helmets led the arrival of reigning kings and queens, princes and princesses—Julie was thrilled to see Princess Grace of Monaco walking with her son, Prince Albert—and then the Spencer family arrived to take their places at the left of the dais. Despite the organ music, the crowds outside could be heard cheering with renewed frenzy as bands along the route played the national anthem. Nick informed Julie that the queen and the royal family must be arriving in their carriages. At some signal, everyone stood up and, led by the lord mayor in ermine-trimmed robes and carrying the Pearl Sword, Queen Elizabeth passed within feet of Julie, wearing aquamarine, the Queen Mother in pale green, the Duke of Edinburgh in full uniform, and Princess Anne looking gorgeous in white trimmed with yellow flowers that matched her tiny veiled hat.

The cheers outside grew even louder to announce the arrival of the bridegroom, but in the cathedral the atmosphere subtly altered to one of solemnity as the organ burst into a trumpet tune and Prince Charles walked slowly down the red carpet accompanied by his two brothers. The congregation's whispering had stopped now, so everyone heard the renewed cheers and the great roar of delight that greeted the bride's arrival.

Trumpets brayed a fanfare while an expectant hush descended. Julie longed to look around to get a first glimpse of Lady Diana, but didn't dare. The organ broke into a voluntary and she knew that the bride had begun her slow, three-and-a-half-minute walk to meet her bridegroom, but only when a flash of white appeared on the edge of her sight did she dare glance to the side to see Lady Diana, clad in yards of flowing veil and a crinoline dress of flounced ivory taffeta, come past on the arm of her father, the earl. Behind her an embroidered train flowed romantically for yards, carried by the smallest bridesmaids, who also wore ivory satin with gold sashes and slippers, and carried baskets filled with flowers that matched the flower garlands in their hair. It was like something out of a storybook, almost too beautiful to be true, and though Julie clamped her teeth on her lip, her eyes stung with emotion.

All through the service, hearing the two young people make their solemn vows, Julie fought to keep her emotions under control and tried to rid her mind of dreams of herself and Nick in those central roles. She caught her breath when Lady Diana reversed the names of the prince, " . . . Philip Charles Arthur George. . . ." But a moment later, Charles himself made a slip—endowing his bride with all his "goods," rather than "worldly goods." A glow of affection for the royal couple warmed Julie at these very human little errors.

But when the archbishop began to intone, "Those whom God hath joined together let no man put asunder," a tear escaped to plop down her face and wet the pink silk jacket.

Beside her, Nick silently offered a large white handkerchief, and when she glanced up to give him a wobbly smile, she saw that his own eyes were none too dry. He smiled ruefully and clasped his fingers with hers, holding her tightly as if for mutual comfort.

He retained hold of her hand even when the congregation sat down to listen to the choir sing an anthem. The deeply devotional part of the service continued, and soon the bridal pair moved toward the high altar for prayers to be spoken as their marriage was blessed. There followed a crash of drums at which the congregation rose to its feet to sing "God Save the Queen," with a fervor that raised the hairs on the back of Julie's neck. The great cathedral seemed filled with a spirit of patriotism mingled with love and affection, an almost tangible thing that filled Julie with choked wonder.

But it was so hot! Under the TV lights everyone had begun to sweat, and on the edge of Julie's vision a fan fluttered—she fancied it was cooling the plump brown face of the massive king of Tonga. Another odd little note was struck by the linen bags that kept descending on strings from some aerie, holding precious cans of exposed film, and way up in the dome photographers and TV cameras were dangling from the roof on safety harnesses.

While the main protagonists moved offstage to sign the registers—and possibly to mop their brows—a musical treat waited as the orchestra struck up and the golden voice of the Maori opera singer Kiri Te Kanawa soared around the spaces of the cathedral, top notes lingering in the dome to add another spine-tingle to the experience. The mood changed once again, to rejoicing, as the massed choirs joined their voices to the celebration, and very soon Prince Charles and his bride emerged from the side chapel to a fanfare of trumpets from the Whispering Gallery, which must have deafened those suspended photographers.

Pausing to acknowledge their respects to the queen, the newly wedded pair came on down the aisle, smiling. The bride's veil had been thrown back, her beauty and happiness undisguised as she leaned on her husband's arm to the accompaniment of the "Pomp and Circumstance" march. Her bouquet was a waterfall of green and white, with touches of yellow, against the fairy-tale sparkling gown, and the prince in his full-dress naval uniform smiled proudly. Behind them came their attendants, the bridesmaids enchanting in their puffed dresses and flowered garlands, while the two young pages looked suitably grave in Victorian naval uniform. Then came the families, all seeming delighted that the occasion had lived up to every expectation.

A cheer surpassing all the rest could be heard as the Prince and Princess of Wales made their appearance in front of the crowds waiting outside, and from above, the bells began to peel out the joyful news that the marriage had taken place. Julie looked ruefully at the soaking handkerchief in her hand, catching Nick's eye to share a smile with him that only made her weep again.

They had to wait until the VIPs had departed, of

course, then slowly the humbler guests began to leave the cathedral, relieved to be away from the heat and able to breathe fresh air, but still stunned by the historic splendor they had witnessed.

"I'm afraid I shall have to give lunch a miss," Nick said as the Rolls Royce slid up to the curb. "You go with mother and Serena, Julie. I really want to get changed and be out among the crowds. I've already missed too much."

"Yes, but Nick—" his mother protested.

"It's work," he told her. "I'm sorry, but you know how it is. You go ahead. I'll find a taxi somewhere. Give my apologies to the Smyth-Howards." Touching Julie's arm, he added to her, "I'll see you at the flat this evening," and was gone, loping off among the gaggle of departing guests, some of whom had been stopped by radio and TV interviewers.

It appeared that the Smyth-Howards, friends of the Ardons, had organized a lunch party at one of the top hotels, and it had been assumed that Julie would join them.

"Now don't you let me down, too, Julie," Lady Ardon pleaded. "We shan't be all that long, but it would be such an anticlimax for you to rush straight back to work. Do come and have lunch with us. I'm sure we all need a meal."

Julie forced a smile and agreed. Lady Ardon was right about anticlimax. When the moment came for her to return to work, it would be the beginning of the end of her trip to London.

The lunch party took place in a private room at the hotel, where several TV sets relayed pictures of the crowd gathering around Buckingham Palace and filling The Mall by the hundreds of thousands. Perhaps forty guests attended the lunch, but a good deal of their attention was on the TV coverage as the wedding party made several appearances on the balcony to wave to the ecstatic crowds, who went wild when Prince Charles kissed his bride. Every detail of the wedding was discussed, and everyone agreed that

Lady Diana—or the Princess of Wales, as they must now learn to call her—had made a perfectly stunning bride.

Eventually, Julie and Serena took a taxi back to Kensington, but such was the crush of people and traffic that it was almost four o'clock before they arrived at Nick's apartment, and then Serena insisted that Julie must stay and watch the bride and groom depart on their honeymoon. So the television went on again, showing some studio party, which was interrupted when cameras were switched again to the palace to show the prince, now wearing a gray lounge suit, and his princess, in salmon-pink with a saucy little tricorn hat, drive off in a landau with a mounted escort. Julie and Serena laughed over the mass of balloons bobbing behind the carriage, blue and silver with the Prince of Wales feathers on them, and the homemade sign reading Just Married, which, according to the commentator, had been put there by the joker Prince Andrew.

"They look so happy," Serena sighed, mopping her eyes yet again.

"Uh-huh," Julie agreed, unable to say more because her own throat was thick with tears. She was happy for the handsome couple smiling from the TV screen, but for herself there was only a cloud of sadness waiting to engulf her.

At last she forced herself to face reality, which meant changing out of her pretty wedding outfit into something more suitable for a last working visit to International Press. To write her last article on the wedding. On her last day in London. Before her last evening with Nick.

The ceremony, as well as everything that surrounded it, was so fresh in her mind that she was able to describe it in detail, exactly as she had witnessed it. The office was in uproar that evening as every correspondent wrote his own wedding story, and she caught only a glimpse of Jim Dawes. Maddie Venables had taken the day off. She would write to them and thank them for their help, Julie thought. Face-to-face good-byes might have been more than she could stand right now.

Mid-evening she took another taxi through the still-celebrating crowds, trying not to think that this was her last taxi ride in London. Suddenly she was doing everything for the last time, and it would all culminate in the painful wrench of taking leave of Nick. Already she was steeling herself not to show him just how unhappy she felt at the prospect.

As she left the elevator, he opened the apartment door and smiled at her. "All done? Good, then you've just got time to get ready. Serena's gone out with Adrian again. Have you enjoyed your day?"

"It's been . . . oh, words can't describe it!" She walked past him, throwing out her hands eloquently. "There'll never be another day like it."

"Not in our lifetime, anyway," Nick agreed. "I always thought fairy stories were corny, but when you actually see one take place in front of your eyes, involving people you know—"

Turning, she faced him squarely, a little frown between her brows. "Yes, even you found it quite moving, didn't you? In spite of all those sour remarks."

"Oh . . ." He shrugged, a corner of his mouth lifting slightly. "I wasn't entirely serious. I did it mainly to annoy you, though ever since their engagement was announced, I've imagined how I might feel in the prince's shoes. Personally, I'd have hated all the fuss and publicity."

"But the prince is used to it," she argued. "He said himself he's been raised to it since boyhood. It's all part of being who he is."

"Even so, he's a human being, and so is Diana. I hope the media will leave them alone for a few days now. Honeymoons are supposed to be private affairs. I know I wouldn't fancy having cameramen chasing me while I was trying to have a few days alone with my bride. Would you?"

She shook her head, more foolish tears choking her. If she were on a honeymoon with Nick she would want to be completely alone with him, but that was a subject she had been trying to avoid all day.

"I'll go and have a shower," she muttered, and swiftly left his presence.

She put on the pink silk she had worn earlier, letting her hair flow down in shining gold waves. One last evening was all she had left of this magical visit to England, but she wouldn't think about that. Tonight she would take each moment and cherish it to remember for the rest of her life.

"Are you ready?" Nick called through the door. "The taxi's here."

She went out into the little hall, trying to contain the trembling of her muscles as she saw him waiting, wearing a dark lounge suit and white shirt. Whatever he wore he looked marvelous, she thought. Faded jeans to elegant morning dress, Nick was the most attractive man she had ever known. She had a feeling that knowing him was going to jaundice her opinion of every other man she might meet.

Beneath a sky streaked with gold from the sunset, they rode in the black taxi through streets where people still celebrated the wedding. Laughing groups danced to the music of street musicians or wandered arm in arm as the taxi moved through streams of other traffic, following the route the honeymooners had taken, past Big Ben and the Houses of Parliament and across Westminster Bridge.

Eventually the taxi stopped among the modern concrete walkways and elevated paths behind a huge complex building that Julie knew from the signs must be the Royal Festival Hall. Nick paid the taxi driver and then put his hand under Julie's elbow to guide her around the building and up a flight of steps to a building fronted by a flagged area, edged by trees. Across the river, the city spread out, reflected in the water.

"I was lucky to get a table here," he said. "They'd had a cancellation. There's a ballet being performed tonight, and after the show the restaurant will be crammed."

Through a vast lobby they came to an elevator and rode up to another level, where glass walls gave views over the river and where lounge bars waited for customers. Up a broad, deep-carpeted stairway they came to the glass-walled Riverside Restaurant, a huge room with tables spread with pink cloths. Cathedral-like spaces, beneath a high ceiling supported by white pillars, swallowed the voices of the diners, giving the place a hushed, intimate atmosphere.

The head waiter showed them to a table for two by the window, which gave an almost unobstructed view of the river and the city beyond. A single carnation graced the table, with a lamp bowing its head to illuminate their meal.

Studying the menu, Julie ordered hors d'oeuvres to be followed by veal piccata, and while Nick mulled over the wine list, she gazed at the view outside. Stark rectangular lamps beamed out across the walkway below, making dashes along the Embankment, and beyond them more lights were strung out by the riverside behind the trees. To the left, golden lamps hung along a bridge that spanned the river, leading her eye to the opposite bank, where mellow floodlights lit some of the buildings, their reflections dancing in the water. She recognized an illuminated red circle as the position of a subway station, and from a tall tower in the distance another red light winked on and off, while elsewhere a ball of light on another building seemed to be revolving.

She would always remember London by night, she thought. Each time she saw city lights it would remind her of Nick. But she mustn't think that way, it only made tears lap harder against the barrier she had erected.

As they ate, he pointed out various landmarks of the city across the skyline, where stark modern blocks were softened by the domes and crenellations of the past. In the center of her view lay the Shell-Mex Building—a square head and shoulders with a floodlit clock for a face. The clock's hands marked off the minutes of her last evening. Nine-thirty. Nine-fifty-five. She began to hate that clock.

"Would you say you had enjoyed your visit?" Nick asked, breaking into her reverie.

"Oh, yes!" Her voice came light and breathy. "Yes, it's been fantastic. I don't know how to thank you, Nick. You've been—"

"That's not necessary," he broke in, stopping her with an abrupt wave of a hand. His shirt cuff gleamed very white in the glow of the table lamp, but his face was more shadowed, wearing a somber look that caught at her heart. "I suppose you'll be looking forward to going home."

She took a deep, shuddering breath and replied honestly, "I'm not. But then it's all been like a dream, and I have to wake up sometime. You can't live on a high for ever."

"There'll be other assignments," he reminded her. "Oh, nothing quite like this, I don't suppose, but probably even more satisfying, professionally. Now that you've proved yourself, the sky's the limit."

"Yes, I guess so," she said, then turned to gaze out of the window again, afraid of revealing what she was feeling.

A train rumbled over the bridge, sliding invisibly through the night. Shadowy figures passed on the walkway below, and beneath one of the trees a couple stood entwined as a boat slipped silently beneath the bridge, ruffling the shimmering calm of the Thames.

She became aware of a distant trumpet, tuneful but melancholy, wooing pennies from passersby. Its lonely sound echoed her own emptiness.

"Is that what you really want?" Nick asked quietly. "A career as a journalist?"

Turning great green eyes to his, she sighed. "I thought so. Now I'm not so sure."

"Oh?" An eyebrow quirked in surprise. "But you were so keen to do well."

"Of course I was! Hank Freeman expected me to make a mess of it, and Jim Dawes didn't believe I could

175

handle it. I had to prove them wrong. And there was my family—an Elliott is expected to be tops. They didn't approve of the career I chose, but once they'd recovered from the shock, they assumed I'd be brilliant at it. All the Elliotts are brilliant. Well, I've done it, haven't I? I've shown them all what a success I can be. But *I* know it wasn't because of my talent—it was because of you and because I fell in love with London and this whole impossible wedding thing. I'm not a great reporter. I never will be. Maybe I ought to quit while I'm ahead."

He watched her, frowning slightly, his eyes full of questions. "I've obviously misunderstood. I thought you were superambitious. So what will you do instead?"

"Who knows?" she said, shrugging. "Do the conventional thing, I guess. Get married. Raise a family. That's what Elliott women are supposed to do. Maybe I'll do free-lance writing in my spare time."

Unable to bear looking at him, she stared again across the river, seeing the clock that moved inexorably past ten-thirty. Round lights in the high ceiling of the restaurant reflected on the window against the dome of darkness outside, like a hundred stars in regimented rows, and she was suddenly aware that their own table was reflected there, too, a sharper picture against the rippling river. She let her eyes dwell on the image of Nick's dark head and classic profile, seeing it shimmer through her tears.

"Would you like some dessert, sir?" came the voice of the waiter.

"No, not for me," Julie said swiftly, her eyes briefly meeting Nick's before she returned to her contemplation of the river, hoping to hide her sadness.

"Just coffee, thank you," Nick said, and the waiter departed.

Somewhere not far away, that lone trumpeter played the slow cadences of "Yesterday" and as the words rang in Julie's head, the tide of tears swelled higher. As if in a dream she saw the reflected Nick reach across the table, laying a warm hand over hers, his thumb caressing her knuckles.

"What's wrong, Julie?"

"Nothing." She shook her head wildly, swallowing to get rid of the huskiness in her voice. But as she glanced at him a tear spilled down her cheek, betraying her. "I just hate the thought of leaving, that's all. I've been watching that darn clock, wishing it would stop."

"So have I," he said.

She blinked in incomprehension, for from where he sat he could not easily see the Shell-Mex clock. Then Nick pointed behind her, and she turned and saw, beyond her shoulder, the illuminated face of Big Ben.

His hand tightened around hers, drawing her attention back to him, and in his eyes she read a sorrow that equaled her own, and a sudden hopeful pleading. "You don't have to go back tomorrow, do you? You could cancel the flight. Don't go, Julie. Stay with me."

Her eyes dimmed, and a roaring came in her ears. Faintly she was aware of the waiter arriving with the coffee, but neither she nor Nick took notice of the man. They looked into each other's eyes, held immobile by what flared between them too strongly now to be denied.

"What about Liz Bentham?" she managed.

He shook his head slightly. "All that was over a year ago."

"A year? But—"

His other hand came to unclench hers and lay it between his palms with a firm, consoling pressure that was also an apology.

"You have to understand, Julie. . . . After Liz and I broke up, I swore never to get involved with anyone again. And then you came along, pretending to be so tough, when all the time you were unsure of yourself. It irritated me at first, and then . . . then it hit me so hard I couldn't believe it. I didn't want to fall in love with you, but it happened, like a bolt from the blue."

"But when I asked you about Liz, you didn't deny it."

"I think I said I'd known her for a long time, which is true. And, you know, she wasn't at my flat the day you phoned. That was Serena. I could have told you so, but

177

at the time. . . . I suppose I was still so bewildered by what was happening to me that I needed some sort of barrier. Part of me was annoyed that I'd let you get through my defenses so easily. But what you said—something about being hurt but not letting it stop you believing—you were right. But I still wasn't sure how *you* felt about *me.* You seemed to change every time I saw you, and I was convinced that you were only interested in your career. And then this last week it's been worse than ever, with you staying at my flat. I felt that you were under my protection, and how could I take advantage of that?"

Unsteady laughter sobbed out of her as she began to believe that he meant every word. "Is that why you kept holding back? I thought it was because of Liz Bentham."

"Just because you found some female clothing in my flat?" he asked dryly and, seeing her flush, added, "Serena told me. I didn't even know those damn things were there, or I'd have explained about them."

"It wasn't only that," she said, sighing. "Maddie told me you were almost engaged, and Hal said there'd been talk of marriage between you and Liz. And—and I saw you with her one day, outside the theater one lunchtime. That seemed to confirm it."

"Oh, good grief!" he breathed, lacing his fingers with hers even more firmly. "I took some publicity stills for her a while back—we're civilized enough to stay friends, you know. I met her simply because she needed the pictures in a hurry. And when I walked her to the theater, she kissed me to say thank you and goodbye, since she's off to Hollywood to test for a part. That's all it was. Do you honestly think I could have behaved the way I have done with you if I'd cared about someone else?"

"I guess not," she said, then gave a choked laugh. "Another man might have, but not you. You're old-fashioned."

Another smile twitched at his lips. "Yes, I'm afraid that's true."

"Oh, don't apologize," she said swiftly. "I like it."

"Like me?" he asked in a meaningful tone, an eyebrow lifting.

"Love you," she amended softly. "Don't you know that?"

"I just wanted to hear you say it," Nick said, his expression no longer guarded but bright with a tender passion that made her blood run like warm honey. "Now, let's have this coffee and go before I scandalize London society by kissing you right here."

The ballet must have ended. People began to stream from the concert hall, bright evening gowns and black bow ties flowing down the stairs and through the lobbies beyond the glass walls, some of them coming to fill the restaurant to capacity, though Julie hardly noticed them. She was drowning quite happily in the depths of smiling brown eyes.

Eventually they went out into the mild evening air and climbed the steps to the Hungerford Footbridge, on whose ramparts the trumpeter still played his haunting melodies, with a hat by his feet containing a fair collection of silver, to which Nick added a fifty-pence piece.

In the center of the bridge a semicircular platform reached out above the water. Here Nick stopped, drawing Julie to look at the glittering city, at the curve of the river before them. In the distance was the floodlit dome of Saint Paul's Cathedral, where earlier that day they had witnessed the marriage of Prince Charles and Lady Diana Spencer. Their Royal Highnesses would now be safely at Broadlands, the big country house where they were spending their first two days of married life, but Julie thought that they couldn't be any happier than she and Nick were at that moment.

From his pocket he produced a time-worn ring box, opening it to show her the emerald inside. "It's a family heirloom," he said. "My grandmother, the Dowager Lady Ardon, gave it to me to give to my future wife, but it's been safely locked away until today. Will you wear it for me?"

179

Standing close to him, his dark hair mingling with her gold, she watched dazedly as he slipped the ring onto her finger.

"I'm sorry it's not sapphire and diamonds," he murmured in her ear. "And when we get married there'll be no processions and cheering crowds."

"Thank goodness," she breathed, lifting her lips to his for the first sweet embrace of the rest of their lives.

She would go home before too long, and Nick would go with her, to meet her family. How thrilled the Elliotts would be to have the future Viscount Ardon in their family tree. But with the Thames rippling below and the lights of London around her, Julie knew that for her he would always be just Nick, her friend, her lover, and her husband. Nick, who had made her visit to England into a dream come true.

ABOUT THE AUTHOR

MARY CHRISTOPHER now lives in the ancient cathedral town of Lincoln, England, though she has resided in various places in Britain, as well as Germany.

Mary is happily married, has two teenage sons, and has been a professional writer for ten years, with forty novels published under other names.

She loves the countryside, adores London, and enjoys studying history.

Since she dislikes housework, she has become adept at minimizing chores to allow ample time for her great passion—writing.

CIRCLE OF LOVE

Step out of your world and enter the Circle of Love.

Six new CIRCLE OF LOVE romances are available every month. Here's a preview of the six newest titles, on sale April 15, 1982:

☐ **THE BOTTICELLI MAN** by Alexandra Blakelee (#21515-9 • $1.75)

Young American art student Ursula Stewart stood before Count Enrico Benvoglio in the dazzling Roman sunshine. He opened the door of his chauffeured black Mercedes and whisked her off into the velvet Italian night. His resemblance to a fifteenth-century Botticelli masterpiece was uncanny! But Ursula soon discovered that Enrico was very much a twentieth-century man—and too dangerously seductive for any woman to trust.

☐ **VOICES OF LOVING** by Anne Neville (#21538-8 • $1.75)

Jane Murray fell in love with Max Carstairs the first time she saw the famed actor. But soon tragedy drove Max into a reclusive new identity as a mystery writer. Now, unbelievably, Jane was Max's private secretary, winning his trust, igniting his passion. But she hadn't counted on Margot Copeland, a dazzling, dangerous rival, who would stop at nothing to steal Max's love.

☐ **LOVE'S DREAM** by Christine West (#21514-0 • $1.75)

Sharon's job took her far away from the civilized Australian seacoast to a cattle station in the vast Outback—and to Nat, who tantalized her, yet seemed forever beyond her grasp. Like the land itself, Nat was harsh, overbearing and implacable, challenging Sharon to tame his dauntless spirit and claim her place in his wild heart.